Finding Grace

Other Books By Allie Kensington

A Lady for His Lordship

The Duke's Secret
Besting the Earl
Unmasking the Marquess

Finding Grace

Finding Grace

The Sisters of Cherrywood Manor

BOOK ONE

ALLIE KENSINGTON

CHAPTER ONE

"I wish you didn't have to go, Grace," Harmony said, slumping against the pillows on Grace's bed.

"She doesn't *have* to go, Harmony. Grace is *privileged* to go," Patience said. "And you will have a splendid time with cousin Susan, won't you, Grace?"

Grace looked up from her open trunks. As the eldest of seven girls, she enjoyed conversing with each of her sisters. "I plan to have a wonderful time at cousin Susan's, but I shall miss you both terribly."

"I wish I could come too," Harmony said. "How come cousin Susan only extended the invitation to you and not to all of us?"

"You're not out of the school room yet, Harmony," Patience answered. "Besides this isn't just any visit, it's a *house party*."

"I still don't see why I can't come or why you need to go

"

at Christmas time. It won't be the same without you here at home."

Grace laid a pale blue dress into her trunk. It was the nicest dress she had that she hadn't already given to her twin sisters, Felicity and Faith. When the gown was stowed, Grace went around to the other side of the bed and sat next to Harmony. She put an arm around each of her sisters in turn. "I am going to miss all of you, Harmony. But you're going to have a good time here, and I will be back soon."

"A month isn't *very* soon," Patience said. At fourteen, she was only two years older than Harmony who was the youngest in the family.

"I promise I will bring you back all of the stories of my time away."

Harmony smiled, a lightness coming back into her eyes.

"Don't forget to take note of what's fashionable," Charity said, coming into the room. "I should very much like to know what is in style before the Season begins." Charity was nineteen, and the middle of the seven sisters.

"It is not as if you are going to London right now," Hope said, following her sister into Grace's bedroom. Hope was seventeen.

"I shall do my best to remember everything," Grace said. "And I expect that you will tell me about all of the things I'm missing here. I want to know about the Christmas ball, and anything else that you attend."

Grace's four sisters who were in the room nodded eagerly at the assignment.

Charity went over to the wardrobe, pulling out a cream-colored dress with delicate beadwork on the bodice. "Aren't you going to take this one? It's your favorite."

Grace looked at the gown. Frayed edges on the hem showed just how much the gown had been loved over the last couple of years. It hadn't been a priority to fix the gown, or have it repaired. She smiled at her sister. "I think I will leave that one this time."

"I think you should take it," Charity said, moving towards Grace's trunks as if she had settled the matter herself. "No one looks handsomer than you when you're wearing this gown."

"You look like an angel in it," Harmony said approvingly.

Grace smiled at her sisters, then nodded. "Very well, I will pack that one as well." She accepted the gown from Charity, arranging it in the trunk.

"And what about this one?" Charity asked, holding up yet another gown.

Grace shook her head. "I believe I have enough already." The rest of the gowns in the wardrobe were similar to the ones Charity had just insisted she take. They were practically worn through. The rest of her dresses, which had still been in good repair, had been handed down to her twin sisters just younger than her.

A knock sounded on Grace's bedroom door. "Come in," she said.

Her mother stepped into her room, surveying the scene

before her. "Girls, will you each go finish the preparations we talked about? And Hope, will you fetch Felicity and Faith?" Every daughter in the room curtsied and left the room. Once Grace's sisters left the room, her mom spoke again, "How are your preparations coming along? Mrs. Mead and her daughters should be arriving soon."

Grace peered through her curtains to view the front drive. The sun filtered through a cloudy sky. It would be a beautiful day to travel. "I'm nearly ready."

"Did your sisters help you or just distract you?" Her mother smiled at her, showing she was not the least concerned about it.

"They were helpful. I was just thinking through what I need," she said, glancing once more to her open wardrobe at the old dresses. "I don't suppose I could borrow back the gowns I've given to Felicity and Faith?"

Her mother's face fell, sadness washing over her. "I'm sorry, Grace, but they have Christmas parties that they will also be attending this year, and you know that they are in a much better position than you ..." Her mother cut off what she'd been about to say, and only shook her head sadly. "I'm sorry, my dear."

Grace nodded, putting on a brave face for her mother. "It is quite all right, Mama. Do not fret." She and her cousin, Susan, were of similar size. Perhaps Susan would let her borrow something a little more suitable to a ball than what she had, but she didn't voice her thoughts aloud.

"I do have a small gift I would like to give you," her

mama said, opening a small cloth in her hand and pulling out a small silver comb with blue and green jewels encrusted into the top. She handed it to Grace. "I know it isn't much, still it would be beautiful in your hair."

Grace stared at the beautiful piece that she'd admired so often in her mother's light brown hair. Her mother had said that it had brought her good luck when she was younger, and Grace could scarcely count the days on one hand when she hadn't seen her mother wear it. Her mother wore it on formal occasions and informal ones; to church and to balls; in the house and out in the garden.

Grace turned over the beautiful comb, feeling each ridge and swirl under her fingertips. "Oh, Mama! This is your precious good luck charm. I could never take that from you." A lump formed in Grace's throat as she held the comb in her hand, but held it out to her mother.

Her mother pushed Grace's hands back, folding her fingers around Grace's. "Grace, this has brought me luck all of my life, but I want you to have it. Wear it at the house party."

"Thank you, Mama. I shall pack it carefully and keep it safe." She placed it into her trunk.

Her mother immediately took it out and put it in Grace's light brown hair. "Make sure you wear it, Grace. A treasure is of no value if it isn't used," her mother said.

Grace nodded, noticing how similar she looked to her mother, especially with the comb adorning her own light brown hair. "I will, Mama."

"Your father wishes to bid you farewell before you leave," her mother said softly. "He's waiting for you in his study. I will see that your trunk gets out of the house safely."

Grace hugged her mother. "Thank you, Mama. I am so excited about this house party."

Her mother nodded. "I'm sorry that it's not a Season, like the rest of your friends had several years ago."

Grace cringed at the reminder that almost all of the friends her age had had a Season before they were twenty, had each found handsome, wealthy men to marry, and were all comfortably settled—some with more than one child now. Grace was now almost twenty-four, and thanks to her age had felt that she'd been on the shelf for at least a year, if not longer.

Her focus this past year had been on teaching her younger sisters proper manners, as her twin sisters would be introduced to Society this Season, thanks to the kindness of one of their relations. Grace, however, was "past her prime" for a London Season, and sponsoring three daughters instead of two, was out of the question.

Grace didn't resent her sisters their opportunity to go enjoy a London Season at the age of twenty-one. She'd even given them her best gowns. It was still the right choice, even though she wished she had something less plain to wear to her cousin's house party. It would be fine. She would manage.

And she would be able to enjoy the company of her cousin while her sisters did all of their preparations for their

Season. They'd only be there for the Little Season, but still there was much to prepare, and Grace wondered how her parents were able to scrape together the funds to make such an endeavor possible, when it had never been possible for her.

She knocked on her father's study door. She heard her father's muffled voice say, "Come in," and she entered the study.

Her father sat behind his desk, a ledger in front of him as always, and a few books stacked on the side of his desk next to a candle. The room was small but cheery. There was a bookcase which held several beloved volumes tucked into one corner of the room.

"Good morning, Grace. Today is your big day. Are you finished packing?" her father asked.

"Yes, I am. Mama is seeing to the trunks right now," Grace said. A lump formed in her throat as she took in this room. She was going to miss being at home with her family.

Her father nodded. "Very good. I will be brief as Mrs. Mead should be here soon. We do not want to keep them waiting, do we?"

"Of course not. It is very kind of her to give me a ride to my cousin's house," she answered.

"It is very kind of her, and very fortunate for us that her travel plans coincide with your cousin's house party. I do not think we would be able to spare the carriage for such a long journey in the middle of winter."

"Do not concern yourself about that. I am grateful that I

can bring Honey along. I should miss my morning rides if I didn't have her with me."

Her father nodded distractedly. He looked down at his desk, littered in paper. He closed the ledger and moved a few sheets aside, revealing the actual grain of the wooden desk. "My dear Grace, I have a delicate subject to broach with you."

Grace raised an eyebrow. In one sentence he'd said that he would be brief and in the other he wanted to discuss a delicate subject. Somehow those two didn't seem to go together. "What is it, Papa?" Was something wrong?

"Your sisters are going to London for the Season," her father began.

Grace knew what he was about to say. And she could respond with grace and poise. "Papa, you do not have to apologize for that. I know our family situation, and that a London Season was never possible for me. Mama and I already talked about that. I promise I hold no ill-will against either of you, or my sisters. I am happy for them, and I look forward to hearing about their adventures. Please do not trouble yourself about that."

Her father tapped a folded piece of paper against his desk, but his features softened. "Yes, well ... I am of course glad to hear that, Grace. You've always been one we can count on for stability in your feelings. Your grace is a blessing to both me and your mother, I hope you know that."

"Thank you, Papa," Grace said. "But I am confused. If

that was not the delicate subject you wish to discuss with me, then what is it?"

Her father slumped back into his chair, the weight that appeared on his shoulders making him appear almost a decade older than he actually was. "Only that, the funding from our relatives is not enough to provide both of your sisters with the London Season that they've been anticipating. I do not know how to break the news to them. They may be more hurt by Society than helped if they go and are forced to settle for less material goods while they are there."

"They will not go without each other. They have scarcely been separated from each other's company for more than a few hours at a time, if that."

Her father nodded. "I had hoped that our family situation would have improved by now, but it hasn't."

Grace read between the lines of what her father wasn't saying. He meant that he had expected her to have married by this point, and that her marriage might have brought the family up from their current level of poverty. They weren't so poor. They had enough for their needs, and that was usually enough. But sending two daughters for a London Season was twice the expense. Grace had no doubt that her sisters would make smart matches. They were both very beautiful, and with the connection of their relatives in London, they should be afforded invitations to the best dinner parties and balls. That is, if they were able to sustain the material lifestyle, that her father was currently in doubt about.

Grace swallowed. "How can I help, Papa?"

He shook his head. "There is one way, but I feel very uncomfortable asking it of you."

Grace took in a long, slow breath. He would ask for her dowry money. It wasn't much, she knew it wasn't, but if her sisters were anticipating accepting proposals of marriage during their London Season, then she'd sacrifice for the family. "You may ask, Papa, and I will happily agree to any terms. You know I would. I love my sisters and you and mama so much. I'm happy to do it."

Her father rose from his chair and embraced her. "You are a good girl, Grace."

"My dowry is theirs," she said with conviction. "I do not mind." She already knew that she was on the shelf, that she would only continue to be a burden to her family, and this was the best way that she could help at the moment.

Her father blinked. "My dear, Grace, you do not need to do that."

"Of course, I do, Papa. It is the only way I can help my sisters." She held her head up. Embracing the life of spinsterhood would take some getting used to, she knew that. But she was going to officially enter this new phase of life with the grace that her parents had admired in her since the day she was born.

"Grace, there is another way." Her father held out the

folded paper to her. "You've been given an offer of marriage."

Grace's eyes widened, her fingers trembling as she accepted the piece of paper. "Who has thought to ask after my hand?"

Her father looked uncomfortable. "The Earl of Ipswich. He is a widower, you know. And he was recently inquiring about women who are ... older and still of marriageable age. He plans to return from Spain in the spring."

Grace opened the note and read it, ice filling her insides. She swallowed hard. "Papa, you cannot be serious. I should much rather give my dowry to my sisters than to be wed to the earl. He is likely twice my age, with children nearly as old as I am."

Her father winced. "I know that it is far from ideal. But he is wealthy and has been traveling the continent for some time. He has a library, and artifacts from all around the world. And because he is a widower, he is not looking for a dowry."

Grace narrowed her eyes. "Plenty of widowers still expect a dowry."

"The Earl does not. He is simply looking for a companion."

"Papa, I do not want to marry him," Grace said firmly.

He gave her a sad smile, then let out a sigh as he nodded. "I can understand that."

"But this letter says that he has already chosen to marry me, how can that be?"

"Several families gave news to the earl. Your name came up among others of eligible women. And he has asked for your hand specifically."

Grace drew in a breath. "Papa, I do not like the thought of an arranged marriage. I never have."

"I know you haven't. But think of your sisters. It is most difficult to have the eldest in a family unmarried, resigned to spinsterhood. This will hurt their chances."

Grace could feel tears pricking at the corners of her eyes. "I do not mean to hurt their chances."

Her father patted her arm. "I know you do not. And I have tried to not lay the burden of this at your feet. Your mother and I have tried to recover since making those bad investments." He pushed the ledger further from his arm. "We thought we were doing you and your sisters a favor by giving so much to the lenders. We never considered that we might end up with nothing to show for it."

Grace nodded, sympathizing with her father. Her parents had done the best they could with the information they'd had when it came to investing, but it hadn't been enough. And in so many ways she'd felt the brunt of their ever-lowering status as she tried to keep things as normal and unaffected as possible for the rest of her sisters. She'd always done that, and she knew that she would do it again, no matter the cost to herself. Her mind whirled around, trying to make sense of everything. "Papa, is it simply the draw of me being married generally that has led you to the earl? Or is there another reason you wish me to marry him specifically?"

Her father's smile was sad. "He does not expect a dowry. The amount of financial burden that alone alleviates *is* tremendous. But he also has a desire to marry someone older—and he has agreed to help fund all of your sisters' London Seasons. That is no small thing."

"Indeed it is no small thing." Grace let out a breath. A marriage of convenience to a man twice her age. A loveless match. But a very lucrative match for the rest of her family. Would such a match be better than a life of spinsterhood? Whatever her life situation was, there was truth to the fact that not living under her parents' roof would lessen at least the day-to-day expenses that they spent on her. Add to it the fact that this man did not want a dowry, also eased the financial burdens on her parents.

Her father watched her, not speaking.

Grace closed her eyes for a moment, centering her thoughts. She took a deep breath, resolve for her family filling her. When she opened her eyes and found her father still studying her, she was able to give him a genuine smile. "Spend my dowry on my sisters, or increase their dowry with the sum you would have given for mine."

Her father's eyes widened. "You'll do it?"

She nodded. "I will marry him in the spring when he returns from Spain, if I have not already improved my situation somehow."

"What do you mean?" he asked.

"I mean, perhaps I have more motivation to make my own match at Susan's house party. I shall make sure that the terms of such an arrangement are made to equal this offer, or I shall accept the earl's proposal."

Her father hugged her tightly. "Oh, Grace. How blessed we are to have such a dutiful daughter as our eldest."

Grace nodded. "I will do what I need to for my sisters and my family. Don't worry, Papa. I shall not accept less for you."

The rumbling of carriage wheels sounded outside the study window. Her father pulled open the curtains. "It looks like your carriage is here."

"I shall go down and say goodbye to everyone," she said, giving her father one last hug.

"You're wearing your mother's comb," he said wistfully. He nodded with approval.

"She gave it to me with the hopes it would bring me luck during my travels."

He smiled. "She was wearing that the day I met her."

"I know. That's why she thinks it's lucky. And I would have to agree. You are both perfectly suited for each other."

"Take care of that comb. I shall miss it, not seeing it in your mother's hair every day," he said.

Grace reached up, about to take it out to give it to her father. She didn't want him to be sad while she was gone.

"No, no. Grace, keep it in your hair. She gave it to you," he said lovingly.

"Thank you, Papa." She lifted up on her toes and gave her father a small kiss on the cheek.

"Thank *you*, Grace."

GRACE STEPPED OUT ONTO THE GRAVEL DRIVE OF Cherrywood Manor. Her family surrounded her to say their goodbyes. She said goodbye to her parents first, and then each of her sisters in turn.

"I shall miss you so much," Harmony said. She turned away after giving Grace a quick hug and rubbed her eyes.

"I will miss you too, Harmony."

Patience and Hope brought a small basket forward. "These are for you for your journey," Hope said.

"We packed all of your favorites," Patience added. "And I added in extra jam."

Grace gave them both a hug. "You are both so wonderful. Thank you."

Charity had a small bundle that she gave to Grace. "Extra paper for you so that you will remember to write down what everyone is wearing and when."

Grace smiled at her sister. "I won't forget," she said, and gave Charity a hug.

"What are we going to do without you?" Felicity said.

"It will not be the same without you," Faith said.

"I shall see you before you go to London, will I not?" Grace said. "We shall not be apart long."

Felicity and Faith looked at each other. "We may leave early for London," they both said in unison.

Grace gave them an extra hug. "Then I shall wait to hear how London is, if I do not see you again before you leave."

Soon the trunk was loaded, and Grace tucked her basket and package close to her side. She gave Harmony a final hug. None of her sisters had any idea what she was about to do for all of them.

Her father's words about marriage sunk deep into her. Her sisters huddled together, waving their hands in farewell next to her parents. She waved back, sending up a silent prayer that both Harmony and Patience wouldn't despair for too long while she was away.

Grace's heart squeezed. She loved them all so much. And when she thought of all the ways she'd be helping alleviate her family's financial distress by marrying for convenience, she knew she would do it. She would marry the earl, if she didn't receive a proposal of marriage at the house party.

After a final glance at Cherrywood Manor, and a farewell wave to her family, Grace ascended into the carriage, and sat facing rearward between Mrs. Mead's two younger daughters. They were eleven and fourteen. Grace talked with them, listening to Mrs. Mead give advice and guidance to all of her children, including the one who sat next to her in the forward-facing seat. Grace opened the basket her sisters had packed for her, and shared the sweets and rolls. Inside Grace found a note from her sisters. She opened it and noted the distinct writing styles of each of her sisters as she read the note. She smiled as she finished the encouraging note, and her heart filled again with love for her family as she tucked it safely into her reticule.

After a few hours the conversation around her died down, and she was left to her own thoughts while Mrs. Mead dozed and the girls looked out the windows.

Grace opened her reticule and took out a letter from her cousin. It was the letter with all of the invited guests on the list, and a little about each one of them. She read through the list, wondering which, if any, of these gentlemen would be a better financial match for her family than the Earl of Ipswich.

There was a Baron in attendance, as well as a Viscount. There were several wealthy gentlemen with no titles. And then toward the end she saw the Duke of Norfolk mentioned. The duke was one of Susan's closest neighbors. Susan had mentioned him on several occasions, especially when his wife had passed away a few years previous. Grace scanned the note again, but there was no mention of a Duchess of Norfolk, so she knew he'd not remarried. Susan had also written and said there were complications in the guest list and that she would provide more details when Grace arrived. Perhaps there were more attending the house party than Susan had mentioned.

Grace circled the Duke of Norfolk's name with her finger. He was a widower. Would he also consider the prospect of marrying someone without a dowry? Surely, the title of duke would be more impressive than a mere earl to her family, and his wealth would certainly provide just as much if not more to her sisters than the earl would. Susan had mentioned that all of the eligible gentlemen attending the house party were of a reasonable age to be considered for marriage, with the exception of two older gentlemen and two older women invited to help chaperone the events.

Grace folded the letter back into her reticule, trying to recall all of the details about the Duke of Norfolk that she'd heard over the years. She'd remembered that Susan had said he was a superior dancer. And, she herself, was an expert in her own right. Perhaps, because he was a widower, she'd have a chance with him. Perhaps he would be a better match for her than an old earl who spent his time abroad, with children not too much younger than she.

She tilted her head back against the carriage and let the bumps of the road soothe her. By the time she reached her cousin's house in a few days, she'd make sure she had a plan to win the duke. He would propose before the house party finished, and after banns had been read, they could easily be married soon after Epiphany.

Everything would go perfectly. She was going to win him, because he was the one that could rival the earl's offer. No other would do. Grace Campbell—the Duchess of Norfolk, had a nice ring to it. She giggled like a school girl who practiced how other surnames sounded with her

Christian name. She didn't know the duke's surname. She'd have to find that out first.

Grace was resolved. She would find a way to marry the duke, save her family, and help provide everything that they needed, so they could choose who they married. She would sacrifice for her family, no matter what the personal cost. She would be happy knowing that her sisters could marry for love because of her. She was being a blessing to them and their future happiness, and alleviating a large burden from her parents.

Grace leaned her head against the back of the carriage, her thoughts swirling around everything she hoped the Duke of Norfolk would be. The more she thought of him, the more she approved of him, over the Earl of Ipswich.

CHAPTER TWO

G race galloped across the countryside, feeling free from the shackles of her future as she rode ahead, determined to reach her destiny at her own speed. She didn't like the idea of leaving Mrs. Mead and her daughters without speaking to them directly, but she'd left a note explaining her plans with the groomsman who'd helped her mount.

Mrs. Mead had been confined to her bed for the past four days, having taken ill. Her daughters had tended to her, and though Grace had tried to be useful, it had seemed that she was in the way more than she was helpful. After lunch at the inn, she'd gotten word that Mrs. Mead was not well enough to attempt the journey again today. Grace knew what she needed to do. She would ride to her cousin's house.

The groomsmen couldn't be spared but one of them gave her the direction to her cousin's estate. It was but a half-day's ride to her destination, and she could make it long before nightfall. The shortcut the groomsman described would get her there even faster. She'd ridden Honey every afternoon since they'd arrived, exploring the surrounding areas. Confident she could manage the last leg of the journey on her own, she'd put her plan into action.

Since the four-day delay in their journey, most of the time Grace was going to spend with her cousin before the house party began was gone. But it was no matter. She would see her cousin soon.

"I've figured it all out, Honey," Grace said to her mare. "Just watch. We will be at my cousin's house before nightfall. Horseback is a much more comfortable way to cross the country than by carriage, don't you agree?"

The tan-colored animal with a white mane didn't reply to Grace's words, only kept up the pace Grace had set for her. The matter of the trunks still niggled at her. Even if her caravan followed her tomorrow, they'd likely still take another day to get her trunks to her cousin's house. Thankfully, she and her cousin, Susan, were of a similar size, and Grace hoped that she would be able to borrow a few of her dresses until her trunks arrived. She'd stuffed one extra dress in her saddlebag just in case.

The sun momentarily broke through the screen of clouds. It was nice to ride with the sun shining, even if she didn't feel much of its warmth. They rode and with each mile Grace felt freer and more light-hearted than she had in a long time.

"This is the way to see the country," she said, looking at the tree lines and the rolling hills. It was breathtaking. "What is that you say, Honey? You want to know why I am leaving without the carriage? Well it is simple. Mrs. Mead is still very ill, and she is not showing signs of getting better. I did try to help in the situation, but her daughters were adamant that they had everything under control. I was going stir-crazy back at the inn. Do you ever feel like that, Honey?" Grace tilted her head toward the animal, as if she were listening and interpreting all of Honey's responses.

"For myself, I do not prefer carriage travel. Though now it will take a little longer to get my trunks, that is a small inconvenience. Traveling with a companion and her daughters was not my idea of a good time. I should have much preferred to ride. If I had to watch the groomsman ride on you one more day, I was not going to be able to stand it." Grace shuddered. The carriage they'd ridden in was much too small for five persons, even if three of them were younger than she was. But Mrs. Mead had insisted that Grace stay in the carriage instead of riding her mare, as she was sure to "catch cold" if she was out in the winter.

But Grace loved the cool, crisp air. She took in a deep breath and filled her lungs. Then she immediately coughed from the cold air. She pulled her dark blue cloak around her more securely. "I still love the cold air," she said defiantly to the silence around her.

She passed three different crossroads, and she made her way with confidence through each of them, sure she remembered all of the groomsman's directions accurately. There were more carriages on the road as the day progressed, so she cut through the woods, not wanting to attract attention to herself as she was on her own.

"Perhaps riding by myself was not the cleverest of ideas," she admitted to Honey, patting her neck. "But we must press forward unless I want to go completely back to the start."

Grace led her horse through the thick underbrush that paralleled the road, to make sure she was going the right direction. As the sky darkened with more clouds, she tried to make her way back to the road, but there was no path that would let Honey through the trees.

A light snow fell around them, and she adjusted her cloak tighter around her middle. She hadn't expected snow. There had been plenty up North, but it should have been milder down south. Isn't that what everyone had been saying?

The bare trees did nothing to block the snow from falling, and she shivered. She needed to get back to the road, and when she saw a small path in the trees, she took it, knowing it would eventually lead to the main road.

"Oh, do you want to know what my plans are, Honey?" Grace asked her horse, trying to distract herself from her current situation. She paused only briefly, as if waiting for Honey to reply, but the mare remained mute. "I'm going to marry the Duke of Norfolk. That's what I'm going to do. I'm going to be the belle at Susan's house party, and I'm going to win the duke over, and then I won't ever have any problems again. I know Papa loves me, and that he wants what's best for our family. But arranging a marriage to a man almost twice my age who is not the option I want for myself. It's too much. The earl has children who are almost as old as I am. Did I tell you that, Honey?"

The snow came heavier, and picking out the trail wasn't easy. She pulled on the reins, willing the animal to go slower through the woods. Wind howled around her, sounding like wild animals against her ears. She swallowed her fear, not wanting to let Honey know what she thought of their current predicament.

Honey pulled against her, wanting to lead her in a different direction, but Grace held the reins steady and firm, winding through the woods, trying to stay on the path that would lead them back to the main road. She shouldn't have tried going through the woods, but to go back and retrace her path would lose what little daylight was left. She had to press on. She knew she could make it. Her cousin's house couldn't be too far from where they were, especially since she'd taken the shortcut through the woods.

Snow fell in heavier clumps, and she brushed the snow from the top of Honey's head, speaking softly to the animal. Honey's ears twitched, and before Grace could pull on the reins to steady herself, Honey reared, snorting, and bucked Grace from her saddle. She landed on the ground with a slap to her hip and leg, her head jostling with the motion.

Dazed from the fall, she looked up to see Honey running wildly through the trees.

If Grace's pulse could have chased Honey down, Grace would have found the animal in no time, but Honey was now out of her sight, only a trail of hoofprints left in her wake. Grace pulled herself up, gasping when she saw her palms scratched and rough. Scarlet drops of blood fell onto the white blanket of snow in front of her. The same snow that had hidden the rocks she'd landed on. She rubbed at the side of her leg, that would likely be bruised. She took a deep breath.

It was going to be alright. She was going to follow her horse, give Honey a stern talking to for throwing her, and then they'd be on their way to Susan's hopefully before it was too dark. The trees grew closer together as Grace followed the hoofprints for several yards. Soon the trail became harder to traverse. Logs and thorny bushes blocked her way. She went around the obstacles as best she could. She climbed over a particularly large tree that scratched at her dress, tearing some of the fabric. She pulled to yank it free, then tripped over a root hidden from view by the snow.

Unable to grab for something to stabilize her, she landed hard, and her right ankle twisted. She screamed in agony. Snow stung her face and hands, seeping into her clothes before she righted herself. Grace yelped in pain as she tried to stand again, collapsing to the ground and hitting her knee hard against the ground.

Tears stung at the corner of her eyes, but she didn't try

to brush them away as they fell. She was alone, in the woods, chasing after her horse that had thrown her. Pain throbbed from her injured ankle. She looked around for a stick or something she could easily use within reach so that she could stand with assistance. But everything was covered in a blanket of snow. It was impossible to detect if there were sticks or rocks beneath. Her hands began to stiffen as the cold seeped into her. Her ruined gloves were soaked from snow and blood. She wrapped her cloak around her trying to gain her bearings on which way the road was. She'd gotten turned around during her fall. She pulled herself up using a tree trunk and gingerly put only her toes down to the ground on her injured foot. The hopping motion helped to alleviate the pain on her injured foot. But she only made it a few steps before she fell again, this time into a bush.

The wind howled in her ears, creating a sense of urgency. She hoped it was only the wind that howled. But in the distance she heard another call, almost as if an animal answered the wind back.

Fear pricked her heart, panic rising and forcing her to move as fast as she could crawl. She didn't dare attempt standing and walking again. She crawled through the soft snow, her fingers pressing down until they hit mud and leaves underneath. With each passing moment she could feel the layers of her clothing getting more and more wet.

Cold poured through her, numbness becoming a friend to her scratched and bleeding hands. She cried out, calling for Honey, but her voice felt like a whisper through the wind. She called again and again, until she heard the howling again—the howling that didn't sound like wind pounding in her ears.

A dark shadow loomed ahead through the snow. The figure howled and raced toward her.

Grace couldn't contain the scream that came from her, as she turned and leaned on the tree for support. She stood and willed her legs to work as she attempted to run back the way she'd come in the woods, away from the wolf that was now pursuing her. Her prayer was not answered. Her leg gave out under the pain. She heard the wolf behind her, louder now, but as she tripped and hit the ground, a dark, cold welcomed her with deafening silence.

CHAPTER THREE

Oliver followed his dog through the woods, wishing the canine understood the need for a larger path when he was on his steed. But Apollo didn't care much about such things when he was on the hunt. Half an hour ago, a horse had stumbled out of the woods, nearly knocking him and his own horse over. The light mare had a cut across one leg, likely from running through the underbrush. The horse was riderless, but the bulging saddlebags indicated that the horse had started out with a companion.

Oliver had chased after the horse until he caught and pulled on its reins. After speaking soothingly to the animal, he'd tied her up to a tree. The weather had picked up, making it difficult to follow the horses' tracks through the snow when Apollo bounded ahead of him. He'd called to

Apollo hoping the dog would obey his order to come, but Apollo stood still, pointing deeper into the dense forest.

Oliver stopped alongside his dog. "What is it, Apollo?"

The dog responded with a large bark that echoed off the trees. He howled with a fierceness that Oliver only saw when Apollo was on the hunt.

Before he gave the command, Apollo was off again, down a steep part of the woods.

Poseidon neighed, knowing his aim was to follow the dog, but Oliver pulled him to the side. He'd seen where Apollo was headed, but that was no way for his horse to go. Instead he took the overgrown path that wound around the steep slope at a much more gradual slope. He could hear Apollo's barking and howling, though it was faint on the wind. And then he heard another cry. One more indecipherable. Had Apollo found an injured animal?

He urged Poseidon forward, taking care through the snow, until he found Apollo, beside a cloaked figure on the ground. Instinct kicked in as he dismounted, and the dog kept barking. "Good boy, Apollo," Oliver said, rewarding the dog with a pat on his head. Apollo whimpered.

"This must be the horse's lost rider," Oliver said aloud, moving toward the man on the ground. He didn't want to startle him so he said, "Hello, sir. I found your horse. I'm going to help you."

He put his hand forward to touch the man's shoulder, then removed the hood from his head. Panic filled him. "You're not a man." His pulse pounded in his ears at the sight of the young woman. He looked around but there was no sign of anyone else around. Drops of red blood were on the snow around her. He saw a little bit of blood at her temple, but wasn't sure where the rest of it came from. His vision blurred for a moment, everything around him seemed hazy. He couldn't focus. He couldn't fail, but fear threatened to strangle him.

Apollo's barking snapped him out of the daze that engulfed him. He had to help her. He had to save her.

He put a hand in front of her mouth. A small amount of breath came out, and he breathed a sigh of relief. She was alive, but unconscious.

He rolled her lightly onto her back and then saw her scraped hands. There were no other injuries that he could see, though her once beautiful dress had many tears along the bottom. He whistled, and Apollo sat, giving his full attention to his master. "Apollo, we are going home." The dog wagged his tail as if understanding this news with excitement.

Apollo bounded up the steep slope again.

Oliver scooped the woman up in his arms, noting how cold she felt. Dread poured into him, but he couldn't think about possibilities. His focus was on getting her to his house, and getting her warm. That was his only thought.

He cradled her in his arms for a few steps until he was back to where he'd left his horse.

"I'm sorry about this, miss," he said to the unconscious woman, before he changed his grip and moved her up onto his shoulders, like a sack of flour. It was a good thing she was slight. He was able to hold her with ease.

With one hand resting on the small of her back, he grabbed Poseidon's pommel and mounted one handed. He spoke encouragingly to the horse as he repositioned the woman in front of him, holding her with both of his arms.

"I've never been so grateful for an obedient horse," he said to the unconscious woman, as he steered Poseidon up the steep slope with his knees. They took the area slowly. Oliver wasn't sure what injuries she'd sustained, but he wouldn't risk further injury or jostling more than he had to.

When they made it out of the deeper forest, Oliver guided Poseidon back to where he'd tied up the mare to a tree. Holding the woman with one arm, he quickly untied the mare and secured her lead onto his pommel. He didn't risk dismounting and laying the woman on her own horse. And he didn't trust this mare to follow without being tethered to his own horse.

His hunting lodge wasn't far from where they were, only a mile away, but the journey seemed to take too long as he rode with an injured woman in his arms, leading another horse that didn't seem to like being led. Apollo bounded back and forth, running ahead and then running back to Oliver, as if wondering what was taking so long.

He held her cradled in his arms, keeping her close to him, careful not to jostle her as he guided his horse with a very loose grip on the reins. She was beautiful. He'd noticed that through their journey. And he knew that if he'd thought about that much more, it would be a distracting thought that might get him through the storm, and through this misery.

Night fell, though it was hard to judge the precise time in the stormy weather. Wind blasted against them, sending an icy chill into his core. Through the falling snow, he could make out the edge of the clearing.

"We're not far now. We'll be inside soon, and you'll be able to get warm." He knew she likely couldn't hear him, but he'd felt better talking to her through the ride. It had calmed his own fears and concerns about the situation.

Apollo waited by the stable doors, no longer running back and forth.

"Sorry about this again, Miss, but I will have to put you back on my shoulder." He maneuvered her onto his shoulder, and dismounted with care, hoping she wouldn't be more injured from the jostling.

He held onto her securely, then moved toward the stable door. Cradling the woman in his arms as he did, he wasn't sure how to get the stable doors open with just one hand. The doors stuck, unwilling to budge. He pulled with more force, unwilling to set the woman down in the snow to use both hands. She groaned in pain but didn't open her eyes. "What am I to do?" he asked his question aloud.

He needed to get her inside as quickly as possible, but he had to stable the horses first. He trusted Poseidon to stay where he was put, but he didn't think her horse was trustworthy at all. After all, it was likely the horse's fault that she had been left injured and unconscious in the woods.

At the bottom corner of the door, he scuffed his boot, removing some of the snow away from door.

The woman stirred, moaned and with a flash her eyes fluttered open, a wild look in her light brown eyes. He felt her body tense with fear. She looked around, dazed and confused. He knew he had to allay her fears before she screamed and startled the animals.

He spoke softly, like he had earlier to her spooked horse. "My name is Ollie," he said, unsure why he'd decided to introduce himself by his childhood pet name. Perhaps it was because it had always sounded less intimidating than his formal title. "I'm trying to help you, miss. You fainted in the woods." It was a silly thing to say, but it was all he could think of as he looked at the beautiful woman in his arms. During their journey through the woods and the snow, he'd wondered what color her eyes were. And now the mystery was solved. The color almost matching the shade of her hair. They contrasted beautifully against her dark lashes.

She didn't say anything, so he kept talking.

"We're going to go inside the stable once I can get the door open," he said, scuffing his boot hard against the frozen snow. A blast of cold wind clawed at his skin. He could only imagine she was colder than he was.

"Please do not drop me in the snow." Her voice was hoarse, and she pressed in closer to him.

He wanted to laugh at that statement. "I will not drop you. I am carrying you into shelter. But I am going to put you down so I can open the stable door properly."

He held onto her as he gently put her feet on the ground. "Are you steady?"

"I am no wilting daisy," she said firmly.

He reached for the stable door. As his fingers wrapped around the latch, he saw the woman fall. He lunged toward her, trying to catch her, but she fell to the ground into a large pile of snow.

"Oh!" She cried out, her hands going immediately to her right leg, then she blinked up at him. "You dropped me!" Her voice carried with such energy that no one would have guessed she'd recently been unconscious.

"I promise I didn't mean for you to fall. Here let me assist you." He helped her stand, wrapping his arm around her waist to support her weight. She leaned on him heavily. "Easy does it." He pulled hard on the latch, removing the snow that had been lodged on it. It opened with a creaking. Swinging the doors wide, he pulled on Poseidon's reins, and the horse went into the stable, guiding the tan-colored horse that was still tethered to him.

Oliver quickly brought her inside the stable and set her down on a pile of fresh hay.

She arched an eyebrow at him.

"I will take care of the horses quickly," he said. "I assume this one is yours." He pointed to the horse beside his own and undid the knot that had kept them together. He led both horses to their stalls.

Her voice was soft as she said, "You found Honey.

Honey, we are going to have a very serious talk about you throwing riders in the woods."

Oliver's throat constricted. Horse accidents could be serious. "She threw you? How did you land?"

"On the side of my leg, mostly." Her teeth chattered between each word.

"Does anything else hurt?" he asked as he made quick work of feeding the animals and taking off their saddles.

"Everything hurts right now," she said, looking at her palms, her face drawn in lines of pain.

"We need to get you inside, next to a fire so you can warm up."

She attempted to stand, but cried out in pain again.

"Here, let me be of service," he said, putting his arms around the small of her waist again. She was shivering. "If you'll allow me to carry you again, we will make it to the house much faster."

She let out a breath. "This is hardly proper to be carried," she said, after Oliver had helped her outside and closed the stable door behind them.

There was nothing to be had for it. She couldn't walk, and he wanted to make sure that she was out of this weather as soon as possible. "I won't tell if you don't."

"I am sure I can manage." She tried for a moment, but she moaned with each step.

"May I?"

She nodded her consent.

He picked her up and carried her from the stable the rest of the way to the hunting lodge.

He supported her weight as he opened the front door. Then he picked her up again and set her on the settee. He brought her a blanket and settled it around her shoulders.

He took a few logs and put them in the fireplace and began building a fire. "We need to get you into dry clothes. You've been wet for too long."

She shivered. "Please don't sound like Mrs. Mead who would tell me that I'm going to catch cold by riding a horse."

"No, but you may get something worse. Pneumonia can be deadly. You must get dry."

She looked around, as if taking in her surroundings for the first time. "Are we the only ones here?"

He nodded slowly, then stoked the fire until it roared to life.

"I need to get into town. My cousins are expecting me, and ... this is not proper at all." Panic settled in her eyes, but her whole body continued to shiver.

He held his palms facing toward her. "You've been hurt, and you need to warm up. I promise I am a man of honor. Do you have a change of clothes in your saddlebag?"

"Only a day dress."

As the fire crackled against the wood, Oliver stepped away from the flame and heat began filling the room.

"I shall retrieve your dress and return in a moment." He hurried outside to the stable and grabbed the saddlebag. He was about to close the stable door when Apollo started whimpering. The dog didn't want to be left in the stable, so Oliver whistled and Apollo followed him, wagging his tail excitedly.

Oliver reentered the house, and Apollo bounded in behind him. The woman screamed, hiding behind the blanket.

"Apollo, sit," he said, and the dog immediately obeyed, his tongue lolling out of his mouth as if he was the happiest animal in the world to listen to his master.

She clutched her hand to her chest. "I was fearful of the wolf in the woods, but it appears it may have been your dog."

Oliver rubbed Apollo behind the ears. "He's harmless, just a little on the excited side when meeting new people. He's the one that found you."

She gave the dog a wan smile. "I am grateful for your help," she said to the dog with all sincerity.

"I helped too," he said, not sure why he was jealous of the praise given to his dog.

She looked up at him, an eyebrow arched. "As I recall, you dropped me in the snow after I specifically told you not to."

His lips twitched. "I already explained that I did not mean to drop you."

"So you admit that you *did*, in fact, drop me."

He chuckled. "I apologize again, most profusely. We should hang your cloak by the fire."

She moved the blanket and shivered. She worked with

the small clasp at her neck, and finally was able to undo it. "Where are we?"

"In the northwest corner of Peterboro."

"How far is that from Downham?"

Oliver's heart thudded at the name. "Nearly twenty miles."

"Twenty more miles! I am still so far from my destination."

"Where are you going to?"

"My relatives live in Downham."

"Why are you out here unaccompanied?"

"I was traveling accompanied with another family. We were making fine time and only had another day's journey to go, I thought. Mrs. Mead became ill so we stayed at an inn for an extra four days. I gave a note to the groomsman to let them know I'd gone on ahead. The groomsman gave me instructions, but he said it was only ten miles from where we were. That was barely an afternoon ride away. I would have made it to my cousin's house, I am sure, only my horse was spooked and threw me."

Oliver wondered what had spooked the horse. He hoped it hadn't been his hunting that had done it. Guilt spread through him that he could have been the cause of her injuries. He had to make it up to her. "You look tired. You've had quite the journey. You should get some rest."

"I will rest once I get to my cousin's house. There will be plenty of time when I get there."

"We've established that your destination is twenty miles

from here. Surely, you wouldn't attempt a journey such as that when you are injured, especially by yourself in the dark, and in the middle of a storm." He lifted his eyebrows at her.

"I am quite capable," she said.

"I have no doubt that you are." She was obviously a spitfire. "But that doesn't mean that I as a man of honor can let you go out in such a condition, and in such weather."

Her eyes widened, and she looked around the cottage. "I cannot stay here with you. It would be improper. My reputation would be compromised and I should be forced to marry you, and that wouldn't do at all."

He held back his laugh. She was getting hysterical over nothing. "No one will be sullying your reputation while you are here. I already told you, I'm honorable."

"Yes, but does that actually matter? When the gossip starts I shall be forced to marry you, and then my entire plan will be foiled. Oh this will not do at all." She attempted to stand, but immediately began falling. He reached for her, catching her in his arms.

"You are hurt. You must stay and rest." He held onto her, though she pushed away from him, then winced before falling back onto the settee.

He took her hands in his. Her gloves were soaked and ripped on the palms, dried blood staining gloves and skin. "I am going to help you remove your gloves," he said slowly.

She looked at him with wide eyes. "You're my rescuer, then a stableman. Are you to be my nursemaid now?"

"Unless you prefer Apollo's help to mine."

"I suppose in this case your help is preferable to his."

"With such confidence, I will do my best. Where else are you hurt?"

"It's unladylike to speak of such things."

"I mean to help you."

"You do not understand. This situation ... I cannot stay here."

"I understand perfectly," he said. "And if there was another option, I would suggest it. But you are injured, and you're a woman, traveling alone. I would never turn you out."

"Do you have a neighbor nearby? In the female variety that I could stay with?"

He shook his head. "We are remote here. My closest neighbor is more than eight miles from here. And with the storm, I do not think it wise to be out again tonight."

She huffed out a breath, and in a resigned voice said, "Very well."

"You look exhausted," he said matter-of-factly.

At that she laughed, the corners of her eyes crinkling slightly. "And you must not be married."

A rush of cold, like a shadow pressed in on him. "I am not, but how did you come to think that?" He suddenly felt wary around her. Should he keep his guard up? Could this be a trap to ensnare him into marriage? He couldn't turn her out, even if it was a trick. His conscience wouldn't allow him to do such a thing.

"You just told me I look exhausted. Women, no matter

their state, do not want exhaustion pointed out to them in so frank a manner."

His breathing eased. She was a force to be reckoned with. "I apologize for the unpolished statement of truth."

"I suppose it makes sense when you live so far from others. Conversing with tact is probably not something you are used to." She grinned at him, a glint in her eye.

This woman was positively fiery. Beautiful and fiery. Carrying her and holding her in his arms for so long this evening, he'd thought her as slight and delicate. He didn't think she was frail, though she'd fit easily into his arms when he'd held her on the horse and carried her inside. But he hadn't realized that she was a force to be reckoned with either.

Something stirred inside him. This woman was intriguing in the way she was trying to bait him. Still, he held his tongue, unsure about the motivations of this woman. Traveling alone was highly suspicious behavior, and until he knew more he would not divulge more than he had to.

He focused back on her light brown eyes—the firelight complimenting the beautiful golden color. He knew he had to respond, but somehow the words were sticking to the sides of his throat. "I give you my sincerest apologies, Miss. I only meant to say that after the ordeal you've been through, you should rest. It would be better for you to heal too."

She studied him for a moment, then nodded. "I admit I am more tired than I realized."

"Have you recovered your strength enough to change in the bed chamber?" He didn't want to rush her, but she needed to get out of her wet clothes.

She attempted to stand, but then sank back onto the settee. "I cannot walk. My foot hurts terribly."

"May I help you?" he asked. "I can help you take off your boot..."

She blinked up at him. "I am capable of doing it myself." But after a few attempts she wrapped herself tighter in the blanket. "Very well, you may help me."

He knelt on the floor beside her. He worked at the wet laces, but it was impossible to see what he was doing as she kept pushing her skirts down over her boots. He looked up at her, raising an eyebrow. "Do you want me to help you?"

She pushed her skirts down again, covering her boots. "It is completely improper for you to look at my ankles."

He pressed his lips together. "I am trying to assist you in taking off your boot. I have to look at your boot to help take it off."

"No you don't."

"Have you a better idea on how to accomplish the task?"

She nodded. "Close your eyes."

"You want me to take off your boot without looking?"

She smiled. "Yes."

He shook his head but closed his eyes at her request. Trying to undo the laces without looking was an impossible task.

She laughed. "You are not very skilled at this."

He joined in laughing with her. "It would be easier if I could see." He opened one eye and looked directly into her eyes.

She nodded. "Very well." She clutched her skirts as if she would continue to push them down to cover her boots, but instead she lifted her foot slightly above the hem, wincing as she did. He loosened the laces and pulled and tugged on the boot. She winced and moaned with almost every movement. Once the boot was off he took off her wet stocking, revealing her red and purple foot and ankle. He wasn't sure if it was broken, but it was at the very least sprained. The entire ankle was swollen, but it could have been so much worse.

He looked at her and noticed that she'd been studying him. He put on a brave face, wondering how best to help her with the injury. "I will attend to your hands and your ankle once you have changed into dry clothes."

She nodded, and he lifted her off the settee and into his bed chamber where she'd have privacy to change.

CHAPTER FOUR

After depositing Grace on a chair in his bed chamber, Oliver shut the door and went to work on boiling water for some hot tea. He wasn't exactly sure how to play a nursemaid, but he knew at least getting warm liquid into her would be helpful. He also pulled out bandages and some ointment to help clean the scrapes on her hands. He should also try to get the swelling down on her ankle. He knew something cold would likely help that, but he needed to ensure that she was staying warm first before he subjected her to something cold.

He heard a thump and then a muffled voice. His heart pounded as he made his way toward the closed door. "Miss ..." He paused, suddenly feeling silly for not knowing her name. "Are you quite all right?"

"No, I am not all right, not in the least."

He smiled, she had a fire in her, that much was certain. "Shall I help you?"

She moaned. "Yes, please."

He opened the door slowly and saw her on the floor. "What happened?"

"I tried to get the laces undone. It didn't work."

He averted his eyes. After her hesitancy in helping with her boots, he wasn't sure if he would be useful at all. "I am not sure how I shall help with that."

She sighed. "Shall I ask Apollo instead?"

"I can call him. He's staying by the fire presently."

She smiled. "I am normally quite capable of dressing myself under normal circumstances." She pulled the blanket to her front and angled away from him. "Can you undo the laces? My fingers are too sore and cold to do it."

"Yes, of course." He swallowed. He came toward her and helped her back onto the chair. He swept away the loose strands of her hair around her neck so he didn't pull them. In the process his fingers brushed the back of her neck. Her skin felt like ice. Soft ice.

She shivered as he pulled and tugged on the wet laces, wondering how she managed to get this on or off without a maid. He didn't let his mind wander to anything else, only stayed focused on his task. It was just like helping her with her boot. Except that he wouldn't stay long enough to examine if she had bruises underneath. He closed his eyes to the thought. Finally the laces were loosened enough, and he took a step back.

"I believe that you can do the rest from here," he said.

She took a shallow breath. "Thank you, Ollie."

"You're welcome, Miss. Call for me when you are changed and I will carry you back to the settee." He quickly exited the room, his face hot first from seeing her feet and ankles to touching the smoothness of her back. He shook his head. He was a gentleman, a man of honor in every sense of the word. And she was an unprotected woman at his house. He wouldn't do anything to jeopardize her reputation, or his, for that matter.

He went back to the tea kettle, now full of bubbling water, and poured two cups of tea. He didn't have much to add to the tea as would be customary, but he pulled out some bread and two small pieces of sweet cake. Then he filled another bowl full of clean water. He finished setting everything on the tables next to the settee, when he heard her call from the room.

He found her sitting on the chair, wearing a dry cream-colored day dress. Next to her feet was a heap of wet clothes on the floor. He averted his eyes from her uncovered bare ankles and wrapped a thick blanket around her shoulders. Then picked her up and carried her back to the settee, where she could warm up next to the fire.

"Thank you," she said.

He nodded. "I am happy to help. You shouldn't walk on your ankle while it is swollen." He gave her another blanket, which she rested on her lap.

"And thank you, for earlier—for saving my life."

He handed her a cup of tea. "You're welcome."

She tipped the cup up to her mouth. She only took a few sips and set the cup down, her face lined with pain.

"You should drink more. You need to warm yourself."

She turned over her palms, scratched and caked with dirt and blood. She winced. "I can't."

Oliver pulled his chair closer to the settee, so he was directly in front of her. He took her hands in his, and dipped a clean cloth into the bowl of hot water to clean them.

She winced, shutting her eyes tightly. "It stings."

"I am sorry this pains you. Believe me when I say I do not like inflicting such pain. But it is the best thing for such cuts. It hurts less than an infection would if it is not properly cleaned," he said, ringing out a new cloth in the hot water and gently cleaning each cut as best he could.

"I'm not sure that's very comforting, Ollie," she said.

"It may not be comforting, but it is the truth, Miss ..." He waited for her to fill in her name, but she didn't. "I do apologize that we cannot stand on ceremony, and approach everything properly. But as there is no one to introduce us, perhaps you can tell me your name, so I can address you with something besides miss."

She nodded slowly. "My name is Miss Campbell. It's very nice to meet you, Ollie? That is your name?" She said it like a question.

He smiled. "You may call me Ollie." It kept things much less complicated.

"What kind of name is Ollie anyway?"

He looked up at her. "It is a name my friends call me."

She winced again, her face contorted in pain. "I have never heard it before," she admitted, her words coming out through gritted teeth.

He focused on her fingers, making sure each was clean before applying ointment onto a clean cloth. He touched the cloth to the first cut, and she immediately jerked her hand away.

"Ouch."

"Miss Campbell, shall I tell you about the time I learned to always use an ointment on a cut, no matter the size?" He needed something to keep her mind off the task for at least a few more minutes.

Miss Campbell cringed. "You may tell me any story, as long as I do not have to speak."

He held her hand firmly in his and gently put the ointment on each cut. "I went fishing with a good friend of mine. We were down by the lake, and I wanted to show my friend how perfect the hook could swing around on my pole."

"How old were you?"

"I thought you didn't want to talk."

"I am trying to picture a younger version of you. At which age should I imagine this story? Were you seventeen?"

He chuckled. "I was likely only half that, thank you very much. Around eight or nine."

She took a deep breath. "You may continue."

"I swung the hook around my pole perfectly several times. I am sure I was quite proud of my accomplishment. Until the hook lodged into my leg."

She squinted her eyes, shaking her head. "That sounds very painful."

"It wasn't in the moment. The cut wasn't very deep at all. It didn't even bleed too badly. We removed the hook, and I tied something around the cut to stop the bleeding. Then my friend and I went swimming and fishing the rest of the day."

"Sounds like you did just fine without any ointment." She lifted her brow.

Oliver shook his head. "That is where you are wrong, Miss Campbell. Three days later, I was in bed with a fever, and a very infected leg. My mother and the doctor were not happy when I had told them what had happened. The doctor had to cut away the infection, and though I was lucky and the infection hadn't spread too deeply, it was probably the most physically painful thing I've ever been through."

"That sounds horrible. I suppose I do not want my hands cut off to get rid of the infection," she said with a hint of laughter through her grimace.

"With such lovely hands as yours, they should definitely not be cut off," he said, averting his gaze from her. Had he just admitted aloud that he liked the look and feel of her hands? Even roughed up as they were on the palms, he could tell that her skin was very soft.

He rambled on about his dog and his horse, and asked

about her horse, while he finished cleaning her other hand. He needed a distraction from the curiosity he felt about her. Finally, when he'd finished applying the ointment, he wrapped her hands loosely in bandages. "The ointment takes a long time to soak in. It will keep infections away while your cuts heal, but to prevent it from coming off, the bandages should stay on for the next day."

"That is going to make riding a horse challenging, but I must do what I must do," she said.

"I wouldn't attempt it tomorrow, especially with the state your ankle is in. Is there anything else that hurts? Remember my hook story. Let us not find any cuts getting infected in a few days."

She shook her head, then put a hand to her head. "I think everything else is aches and pains and probably bruises."

He nodded and held out her cup of tea. She held up her bandaged hands. "I do not think these bandages are conducive to drinking tea."

He held the rim of the cup out to her. "Allow me," he said.

Her eyes were locked on his as she accepted the drink. When she was finished he pulled the cup away from her lips.

"Thank you, Ollie," she said softly.

"You are welcome, Miss Campbell." He offered her some of the bread and the sweet cake, feeding her with small bites on a fork until she'd had enough.

"May I ask, what you were doing out in the woods unaccompanied?" He asked the question that had been swimming in the back of his mind.

"I told you I was on my way to my cousin's house. She is hosting a house party in a few days."

"That does not explain why you were unaccompanied."

"Mrs. Mead has not gotten better, but she also did not want me to attend to her, as she had her three daughters with her. The groomsman I asked about the distance assured me that my cousin's house was merely ten miles from where we were. I left a note with him. I knew that Mrs. Mead wouldn't be able to spare her groomsmen when they were ready to depart. But waiting for her to recover—I thought I would have been to my cousin's house long before nightfall. I truly didn't think it was so very far from the Grantham inn."

Oliver whistled. "That is quite far indeed. And you came all the way here alone today?"

She nodded.

"You are either very brave or very foolish," he said.

She held up her bandaged hands. "Perhaps a little of both." She yawned, then put a bandaged hand to her head. "I am much more tired than I realized," she said through another yawn.

Oliver stood up abruptly. "I shall start a fire in the bed chamber. You'll be much more comfortable in the bed than the settee."

"I couldn't. I do not wish to inconvenience you."

"It is no trouble at all. I will be back in a few moments." He left to start the fire. Then he turned down the sheets. On his way out of the room, he took her wet clothes off the floor. "I will hang these up by the fire. They should be dry by morning."

"First you are my rescuer, then my nursemaid, and now my wash maid? Is there anything you do not do?" she asked in a light tone.

"Don't forget I made you tea as well." He smiled at her then began hanging up her dripping clothes.

"You are very accomplished. Though I must say it feels a little awkward that you are taking my clothes like a wash maid," she said.

"It would be even more awkward if you had to put on wet, cold clothes in the morning."

"A fair point," she said.

He surveyed her. Her cheeks were pink, but he couldn't tell if that was because of their conversation or if she was finally warming up. "Do you still feel cold?" he asked her.

"I am much warmer now. Thank you."

He carried her into his room and laid her on the bed. "Is there anything else you require?"

"You have been most kind. I cannot think of anything else I need." The wind shook the windows, rattling and howling with the increase in the storm. Miss Campbell jumped and pulled at the blanket wildly. "Is that a wolf?"

"It is only the wind in the trees and against the glass," he said soothingly. "You are quite safe here."

She nodded, but the look in her eye made Oliver think that she wasn't convinced by his words. His mind raced to think what might calm her. She was a stranger to him. He grabbed a book from his shelf. It was an exhaustive work on the native plants and animals of the area. He cleared his throat. "Sometimes it is hard to sleep when you are in pain." He didn't want to draw attention to the fear he'd seen in her eyes at the sounds from outside. "Shall I read to you? I must warn you that I read very dully when I read aloud. It may help you fall asleep."

She laughed. "You read dully? On purpose?"

He shrugged. At least she'd laughed, even if it was at his expense. He pulled the covers over her, and added an extra blanket on top of her. "Your comb is still in your hair. May I help you with it?"

"You may. And there are half a dozen pins that are holding the rest of my hair."

He hesitated. The large silver comb in her hair would likely cause her discomfort as she slept and as it was visible, it was easy to remove. But finding pins in her hair was an entirely different matter. He gently pulled out the comb and placed it on the side table next to the bed.

"The pins are easy enough to find," she said, then explained the location of each with enough precision that he was able to take them out without letting his fingers linger too long on her soft tresses.

"I'll be out on the settee, if you need anything, just call for me."

She leaned her head back against the pillows. "And you will read to me?"

"Of course." He took the book from the side table. He'd completely forgotten about his offer to read to her. He pulled his small chair closer to the bed. "I will read you the exciting tales of the exotic fauna and flora found in these parts of our beautiful country. And if you stay awake through that, I might even get as far as reading about the animals, which can be even more exciting."

"Very well," she said.

Oliver exaggerated his hand motions when he opened the book and turned to the first page. He cleared his throat and read in the most monotone voice he could contrive. "In the year of fourteen hundred, the Crown commissioned a …"

"Indeed I shall never sleep a wink with such excitement." She laughed.

"I told you, I have a dull reading voice." He smiled at her. "Close your eyes and try to rest. It has been a long day. I will read to you until you are asleep."

"That's how the book starts? It is not quite a story, is it?" She looked toward the book.

He turned the book around, showing her the first page. "This is more of a reference book than a storybook. It's perfect for falling asleep.

"Thank you. And goodnight, Ollie," Miss Campbell said.

"Sleep well, Miss Campbell," he said, then resumed

reading. "...The Crown commissioned a degree to all landowners to categorize their properties not only from a building standpoint, but also the natural world. This led to the rise of the scholars who would travel from ..."

"Ollie?" Miss Campbell's voice was soft.

"Yes, Miss Campbell?" he asked.

"My friends call me Grace," she said.

"Goodnight, Grace," he said, liking the way her Christian name rolled off his lips. *Grace*. It fit her. He stared at her for a long moment, the dark curls of her hair, framing her face. Her skin was brighter than it had been when he'd carried her home. She took deep, even breaths, and Oliver was captured by the moment.

"Ollie?" she said again, this time her voice was barely a whisper.

"Yes, Grace?"

"Would you read a little more to me?" she asked.

"Of course, Grace," he said, before turning the page and finishing the introduction.

CHAPTER FIVE

Grace awoke completely disoriented. Then all at once everything that happened the day before rushed back to her with the intensity of a storm. Her ankle throbbed and her hands were covered in bandages. No, it hadn't been a dream or a nightmare. At once she felt the panic of yesterday, the coldness that had seeped into her, the animal call she'd heard that had scared her. She could have easily perished in the woods, had Ollie not rescued her.

The very thought filled her with a mixture of emotions. He'd said that she was either very brave or very foolish. Yesterday she'd thought she'd been brave, but now she realized that she was very foolish indeed. But a warmth filled her as she thought about Ollie. He had saved her. His manners were polite and put her at ease, though she originally felt like an intruder being in his house without a chaperone. He had been the perfect gentleman, and had helped her in every way. He had seen to her comfort and her care. She smiled as she remembered the way he'd read about plants in such a dull voice. It was the last thing she could distinctly recall before falling asleep.

She didn't know what time it was, and the covered windows gave no indication of the hour, or if it was still snowing. She heard the wind and then a loud bang. "Hello?" she said into the darkness.

Heavy footfalls sounded and then a knock sounded on the door. "Grace, do you need something?"

She looked around, trying to make sense of the dark room. "I should like to come out, if you please."

He opened the door slowly before stepping inside. Light spilled in through the open doorway. "I am sorry if I disturbed you. I just came in from feeding the horses. Were you trying to get my attention for long?"

That explained the clatter she'd heard. "No. I heard you come back in." She took in the man before her. Ollie was tall and handsome. She'd noticed as much last night.

He came toward her. "How did you sleep?"

She swallowed. The idea of a gentleman asking after her in such an intimate way felt strange. And yet, she knew that he was only asking out of genuine concern. He'd made that very clear last night. "I slept as well as could be expected considering the circumstance."

"That is good to hear," he said. "I wasn't sure how long you would sleep, and I didn't want to disturb you. Poseidon gets a little temperamental if I don't feed him first thing in the morning. And there were a few other chores I had to take care of."

"Poseidon?" Grace asked.

"My horse. He's the hardest-working horse I've ever known. He can out pace any horse with such endurance, and he never seems to tire."

"He's probably never thrown you either," she said.

"I've been thrown before," Ollie said. "But not by him. He's really quite gentle, unless he doesn't get fed. Then he can act very wild." He put one arm under her knees, the other around her shoulders, and picked her up effortlessly.

Grace clung to his neck. He had carried her multiple times yesterday, but she hadn't realized how close they'd been until this moment. He smelled of soap and cedar, a pleasant combination. Her breathing was shallow until he put her down on the settee. "Thank you," she said, her throat suddenly dry from the close contact. Yesterday had been a hazy blur, but today everything was in much sharper focus.

Ollie pulled a blanket over her and seemed to take great care in covering her bare ankles and toes with a significant portion of the fabric. "Are you hungry for some breakfast?"

"I am a little hungry," she said, her stomach growling. She kept a blanket around her shoulders, and Ollie put a pillow underneath her swollen ankle.

"I will be back in a few minutes with some food," he said.

Grace took the opportunity to survey the small cottage while Ollie was in the kitchen. Last night, she hadn't paid too much attention to the details. The style of the rooms dated the cottage to perhaps sixty years ago. The cottage was clean and maintained. The main living space had only a few pieces of furniture for sitting, but all of them seemed in very good repair. There were a few small tables. The large fireplace was already crackling. The cheery blaze filled the room with heat.

Somewhere behind her she knew there was a kitchen, and likely a dining room, though she hadn't seen either. Every window was flanked with heavy draperies that reflected a Georgian style with its bold colors, trimmed with gold. There were a few landscape paintings on the walls, but no portraits in this room.

"I wasn't quite sure what you wanted, but I made you a plate," Ollie said as he entered the room. The plate contained toast, eggs, and pork. The dishes were a beautiful pattern, the china pristine. It wasn't what she'd expected from Ollie at all.

"Thank you," she said, her stomach rumbling at the sight of a meal.

"Do you need help eating?" he asked, eyeing her bandages.

"I will try and manage," she said, her cheeks heating as she remembered how intimate it had felt when he fed her last night. She pushed her bandages away from her fingers and grasped the fork. She pushed through the initial stinging on one of her fingers and began eating.

"I don't suppose you have a carriage," she said between bites.

He tilted his head, studying her. Finally, he answered, "There is no carriage house here, and you've seen the size of my stable. A carriage would not fit."

Grace's cheeks burned. "Oh, I did not mean offense in the question. I only wanted to borrow it to get to my cousin's house."

He smiled at her, leaning back in his chair with ease. "There is no offense taken. I wish I had a carriage here that I could loan you. But as it is, the snow is still falling hard. Even if you were perfectly better from your injuries, I would not attempt going so far by horseback today. Storms like these are storms to be weathered while inside, not outside."

Grace nodded, disappointed that her journey would be delayed. She had hoped Ollie would be able to take her straight to her cousin's house today in a carriage, but now that idea was dashed.

She took a bite of her toast and looked around the room again. "What do you do, Ollie? I mean, during the day, what do you do when you are not rescuing damsels in distress in the woods, and taking care of them after?"

Ollie smiled. "I confess I do not make rescuing a regular part of my routine. Only God does the rescuing, though sometimes all He has is us mere mortals as tools."

A shadow flitted across his face, but in the next instant it was gone, and Grace was left to wonder if she'd only just imagined it.

"So, when you aren't rescuing damsels, you are ..." She let the question hang in the air between them.

He swallowed his bite of food. "I am hunting out here. Yesterday when I came upon you, Apollo had been restless, so we went looking for foxes."

"Did you find any?"

"As it turns out, I completely abandoned hunting when I saw a beautiful riderless horse."

"I am sorry to have thrown off your day in such a way."

Ollie shook his head. "Don't be. I am not. And truly I am grateful that we found you so quickly." Ollie swallowed. "You shouldn't ride off alone like that, especially not in the woods."

She felt the reprimand fully. "I know that now." Silence stretched between them as they continued eating their food. She took the opportunity to study Ollie. His light hair was more blond than brown, though in this light it was a mixture of both. She already knew that he was both tall and strong, but she could see the way his muscles filled out his coat. He was dressed simply, but though the material was coarse, it looked as if each piece had been tailored to fit him. When his striking blue eyes landed on her with such depth, she found it hard to swallow or speak. "So you hunt, and ..."

"And I ride my horse, and I play with my dog," he said. He crossed his booted ankle over his knee and smiled at her, as if they were having afternoon tea together. "What do you do to occupy yourself when you're not riding out alone on a dangerous road?"

"It wasn't dangerous when I started out," she said, the defiance rising in her.

His eyes twinkled, as if he were enjoying the joke at her expense. "I beg to differ. The road is always dangerous to an unaccompanied woman. Just because you didn't know or see the dangers, doesn't make it less dangerous. The weather was truly one of the least of your concerns."

"Touché, Ollie." She lowered her eyes to her plate when the look in his eyes turned intense. She grasped for something else to say, how she should answer his question. "Besides riding Honey, which I dearly love to do, I suppose I do the usual female things. One always has something to accomplish, be it an embroidery or a painting."

Ollie smiled. "I do not have any embroidery here, though I doubt you should use needles with bandaged hands."

They finished breakfast, and Ollie took the plates and brought her another cup of tea. The warmth filled Grace.

"May I look at your hands?" he asked, coming to sit beside her in a chair.

She held out her bandaged hands to him. He took off the bandages and examined the angry red and pink scratches.

"How do they look?" she asked. She'd not dared to remove the wrappings herself.

"I think they could use more ointment," he said warily.

She nodded. "Whatever will keep me from a fish hook infection."

He poured the ointment onto a clean cloth and gently touched each of her scratches, but this time it didn't hurt as much. She moved her hand to her head and winced.

He looked up. "What is the matter?" he asked, but before she had time to respond that it was nothing, he inspected the side of her face. "You have a cut in your hair. How did I not see that yesterday?"

"It is nothing. Just barely a scratch."

"Do you trust me to clean it out?" he asked.

"I do," she said.

"I promise to inflict as little pain as possible," he said, sincerity radiating in his voice.

It was the voice that had lulled her to sleep with such richness. Perhaps he had only been teasing her when he had said that he didn't read well. It was too bad he'd picked such a dull book. His speaking voice was the type that should read Shakespeare or poetry. Perhaps he would let her request a reading this evening. Her cheeks burned at the thought. Of all the nonsensical things she could think, she shook her head at the silly notion and bumped into his hand.

"I'm sorry," she said.

"No, I am sorry. I was trying to be gentle, but there is hair matted into the wound."

"It didn't hurt, I was only distracted," she said, trying her best to hold completely still.

In a matter of minutes, he said, "There. I think that will help," he said. "How is your ankle?"

"It is still quite sore," she admitted.

"I imagine it is," he said. "I will make a remedy for it that my grandmother taught me. But you must give it time to heal. You'll be well enough in no time."

She nodded.

"Perhaps we can do something to take your mind off of your ankle," he said.

"What do you suggest?"

"I have an old checkers set. Are you up for a game?"

"Only if you are not a sore loser," she said.

His lips twitched. "I believe I can hold my own in this game." He set up the board and the pieces on the table next to her. "Let me know which piece you want to move and where, and I will move them for you so you can rest your hands."

They played a few games, talking through their turns. She told him about her childhood and her sisters. He told her a little about his family too. She didn't get many specific details about his family; however he told many adventurous stories involving his horses and his dogs. They talked about their favorite family traditions, and she told him how much she enjoyed singing with her sisters. She usually played the pianoforte while they sang during the holidays.

Apollo came and nudged Grace's hand. "Apollo, you must be on my team. Which piece shall I move next to win this game?"

Ollie laughed. "Apollo is only trained in one type of game—the kind he finds in the woods. He shall not be any help to you."

Grace laughed. "That is quite alright," she said, brushing her bandaged hands down his long coat. "I will claim him for my team anyway."

Apollo panted, then laid his head on Grace's lap for the remainder of the game.

CHAPTER SIX

Grace changed into her day dress that she was using as a night gown. It was not as difficult as it had been yesterday, for which she was grateful. She leaned into one of the posters at the foot of the bed using it for balance, while she climbed into bed. It took a little more maneuvering with her sore hands, but she wanted to try it for herself. By the time she situated herself and drew the covers up to her chin, she was exhausted.

A knock sounded at her door. "Do you need anything?"

The sound of his voice made her smile. "I do not believe so," she said back to him. But then she spotted the shelf of books. She would dearly love to read something, more exhilarating than the book on the natural world and botany he left on the table beside the bed. "Actually, I could use your assistance."

"Is it safe for me to enter?"

Heat rose in her cheeks, and she was grateful he was a gentleman. "I am covered, sir."

He opened the door gingerly, then seeing she was up to her neck in the bed covers, he stepped in a little more boldly. "I am at your command, Grace."

"I wonder if there is a volume that would be suitable for my reading this evening," she said, glancing toward the small bookshelf. She doubted he had a gothic novel or any such thing, but some volume of fiction would be diverting, even if it was an adventure story buried beneath the volumes on the natural world and the scientific journals.

He cleared his throat. "I confess, I do not have the selection or the quantity of books that I should have here." He looked like he'd say more, but he didn't. He crossed the room, scowling at the bookcase.

She wanted to assuage her host. "You have a beautiful collection of books. The spines and the covers—they all look magnificent."

He turned to her. "I confess I am lost when it comes to suggesting books. Most of these are practical for ... this part of the country. In a different home and place, I would collect books differently."

"I can't imagine why you didn't think to buy a whole library, in case you one day stumbled upon a woman in the woods who wanted to read." She smiled at him, showing him she was teasing. "I was hoping for something other than a botany lesson."

He rattled off a few titles, and she was about to give up

on the idea of a book. After all, she felt she could sleep better tonight. Perhaps she didn't need a book after all. "I have a small collection of Shakespeare's sonnets lying around here somewhere," he said, looking rather uncomfortable.

"That would do nicely," she said. "I did not see that one on the shelf."

"I believe I know where it is, I shall be back momentarily." He bowed formally before leaving the room. True to his word, he was scarcely gone from the room before he returned again. A worn red leather-bound volume was tucked in his hand, along with new bandages and ointment.

He looked almost reluctant to hand over the little book and put it down on top of the botany book on the small table. "It will be difficult for you to hold the book and turn the pages after I rewrap your hands. Shall I read to you again tonight?"

"If you wouldn't mind, I would enjoy that," she said.

"I do not mind. But first, let us attend to your hands."

She held out her hands to him, and he gently unwrapped the bandages from her hands.

"Your hands are looking better." He opened the small jar and applied a small amount onto each cut and scrape.

"They hurt less than they did last night." Grace held still as his fingers gently caressed hers. A tingling sensation spread through her hands where he'd touched her, but she couldn't tell if it was simply because he'd applied the ointment or if there was something more.

"Less pain is a good sign. You shall be right as rain in no time." He took care rewrapping her hands, and when he settled into the chair he'd occupied last night, the tingling in her hands stopped.

"Shall I see how your ankle is healing?" He glanced to the end of the bed.

"I would appreciate that," she said.

He moved the covers aside and checked on her ankle. He felt around her ankle and her toes. It was very tender and there were a few places where the pain felt sharp. She did her best to brave the inspection.

"What do you think?" she asked, awaiting his thoughts.

He adjusted the position of the poultice and rewrapped her ankle. Settling the covers over her feet once again, he sat in the chair next to the bed. "I think it will take time. We shall see how it looks in the morning." He picked up the volume of poetry. "Do you have a particular favorite?"

She shook her head, which was still reeling from her ankle and toes being examined. She had plenty of favorite poems, but right now she could not think of a single one. "Turn to a page and begin reading. Sometimes that can be very diverting, especially if it's an unfamiliar one."

His lips twitched, but he took the ribbon out from its marked place. He closed the book and then reopened it, letting it fall open. He frowned at the page. "I do not think I like this game."

"Which one did you pick?"

"It fell open to the page that was previously marked with the ribbon."

"It must be a favorite then," she said encouragingly.

He sighed, flipped a few more pages, and then began reading a different poem.

Grace closed her eyes, not focusing on the specific words, only the cadence of Ollie's voice as he read the poetry with more fervor than he had the book on botany on the previous night. Her intuition had been right. He read with feeling in such a way that captured her.

His voice was commanding, then gentle, full of feeling and passion, as he read words about love and words about loss. She dared one glance toward him as she moved her pillow to be more comfortable. He held the book aloft, but his eyes were not on the pages as he spoke. He'd been reciting the poetry from memory! She closed her eyelids again and listened to each inflection and word he spoke until sleep overtook her.

OLIVER RECITED TWO DOZEN SONNETS, MORE THAN half of them from memory before Grace's breathing changed, and he knew she was fast asleep. He read one more, a tragic one, the first one he'd opened to. It was full of heartbreak and sorrow; loss and loneliness.

He took out the light from the bedroom and pulled his large blankets onto the settee. The small furniture was not meant to be laid on by a man with any kind of height, but he would make the best of it again.

After readying himself for bed, he rubbed the growing whiskers on his chin. He had a small shaving set with him, but normally when he came out into the woods, he was by himself at his hunting lodge. It didn't matter if he went a week or two without shaving. But with Grace around, he'd felt a little more self-conscious about it. Did Grace care that he had a beard? Would she notice if he'd shaved? Would she care? These and other questions rolled around in his head, muddling his mind.

He took the small volume of sonnets and replaced the ribbon into the proper page. He had it memorized by heart, and as he said the words softly in the darkness, Apollo whimpered and laid his head on his master's chest. Oliver patted the dog, scratching him between the ears. "You, my friend, are supposed to be my dog. And you've been spending so much time with Grace."

The dog's soulful eyes stared back at him.

"I suppose I cannot blame you though," Oliver said. "She is rather remarkable, is she not?" He closed his eyes but could not get her out of his mind. He changed positions, trying to get comfortable on the settee, but the tossing and turning lasted for three-quarters of an hour. He sat up and lit a candle. Apollo peacefully slept next to the settee, clearly with nothing on his mind to keep him awake.

Oliver stretched, loosening up his muscles that protested

against the cramped position on the settee. "I'm going to the stable, Apollo."

Apollo didn't wake or respond as Oliver stepped over the dog.

The storm still raged, and Oliver pulled his great coat around him. He ducked his head, trying to avoid the freezing stings of the snow and ice. Once inside the stable, he shook off the snow that had accumulated on him. He lifted the small lantern off its hook and lit the candle in the stable.

The horses whinnied, and Oliver spoke soothingly to them as he looked around the area for the item he needed.

In the corner, there were several sticks. Oliver looked for one about the right size for Grace and pulled it from the stack. The rough wood needed some work, but he was determined to help her.

He sat on a stool and grabbed his knife. Stripping off the outside layer of bark was an easy enough task. He focused on smoothing off any of the rough splinters as he exposed the wood.

Poseidon neighed.

Oliver looked up. "I'm working on a gift for Grace," he said, as if answering the horse's question.

Poseidon stamped, tossing his mane.

"It's not time for food," Oliver said to his horse. "I am only here making a crutch for Grace. She is the woman you helped; you remember."

The horse only neighed more loudly.

Oliver put his knife down, then stood and walked over to Poseidon's stall. He stroked the animal's nose. Oliver sighed. "I apologize for interrupting your sleep. I couldn't sleep either." He pulled a sugar cube from his pocket. Poseidon accepted the treat with a grateful whinny. Honey's ears perked up, and she looked at Oliver expectantly. Oliver pulled a cube out for her.

Oliver returned his attention to the stick. "I read her poetry tonight, Poseidon. Can you imagine that?" Oliver looked up, but Poseidon was paying him no attention now that he had received the desired sugar cube. "I haven't read poetry aloud in ages."

He spent the next hour concentrating on smoothing out the stick. The height was about right, but he would have to size it to her in the morning before he finished it completely. The crutch would do no good if it wasn't precisely the right size. He found another piece of wood, wrapped it and fastened it with a leather strap to the top of the stick.

"What do you think, Poseidon? Will she like it?" Oliver asked, holding the stick out at arm's length and giving it a critical inspection. He hadn't worked on a project like this since he was a boy, and immediately he felt his inadequacy at such a task. It would be functional, especially when he sized it for her, but ... there was something missing.

Oliver stretched his muscles. The idea of sleep had fled from him long ago. He wanted to complete this for Grace, but there were some finishing touches he needed to make.

Sitting back down he started making light marks on the smooth wood.

By the time he was finished, it was almost morning. He fed the horses before leaving the stable and headed back to his lodge. Apollo was in the same position he had been in when he'd left hours before.

Oliver lit the fireplace, then pulled his blanket from the settee to the chair, where he was finally tired enough to sleep.

OLIVER AWOKE TO THE SOUND OF APOLLO WHIMPERING. Opening one eye he saw his dog by the bedroom door, wagging his tail. He made his way over to Apollo, whispering to see if Grace was awake before he opened the door.

"I am dressed," she said.

Oliver opened the door and found Grace on the chair, her night dress folded neatly on the table. "How are you?" he asked.

She smiled brightly at him. "I think I am doing a little bit better. I am still sore."

"That is to be expected, I think."

She nodded, pulling her hair over one shoulder. Waves of curls seemed to tangle together. She glanced into the mirror. "I'm afraid my hair is quite a frightful sight. It is normally not so unruly. But I cannot do a twist with my hands bandaged. I can barely get in and out of my dresses."

He smiled, trying to put her at ease. They were both in an unprecedented situation. "Your hair looks beautiful down."

"It's highly improper to have one's hair down," she said.

"Your secret is safe with me," he said.

"Thank you, Ollie."

"Shall I help you out to the settee? I have a surprise for you."

"A surprise? For me?"

He nodded, then picked her up and carried her to the settee. The crutch leaned against the wing-backed chair, and he brought it toward her. "I made this for you," he said, his pulse racing faster.

Her eyes widened. "You *made* this? For me? When?"

"Last night. It's not quite finished yet. I need to make sure that it's sized for you." He helped her to her feet and wrapped his arm around her, supporting her weight so she didn't have to put extra pressure on her ankle. He tried not to notice how perfectly she fit into his side. He put the top of the crutch to the ground to see how high up the crutch came. It was only about two inches off. He could easily trim the excess off. Grace was the perfect height to fit in his arms.

"You made this last night? Do you not require sleep?"

The question caught Oliver off-guard, and he was momentarily tongue-tied, still thinking of Grace in his arms.

Grace glanced around the room, her gaze falling first to

the settee and then to the chair, which still had Oliver's blanket on it. "You did not sleep because I have displaced you from your bed," she guessed.

Oliver shook his head. "That is not the reason. I only thought it would help you. It is a little too tall, but I will take care of that after breakfast."

Grace sat down on the settee. She held the crutch, turning it around so that the bottom of the crutch touched the floor. "Did you do all of this carving too?" Her fingers traced the designs he'd put at the top of the crutch.

Heat prickled the back of his neck. He wanted to justify his poor craftmanship, but instead he just nodded.

"It's very beautiful, Ollie. Thank you very much."

"You are quite welcome, Grace."

CHAPTER SEVEN

"My ankle is still sore," Grace said, her distress evident. "How am I to dance if I cannot even stand?"

Oliver gave her an encouraging smile. She'd only been using the crutch for a few hours, and already she'd been improving. "The more you rest it, the better off you will be. I daresay in a couple of weeks ..."

"A couple of weeks? That is not good at all. I need to be dancing before a few weeks from now," Grace said, rubbing the side of her face. "What am I to do?"

"There will be plenty of other dances. What does it matter if you miss a few dances during the house party?"

"You don't understand," she murmured.

"No, I do not understand why dancing is more important than your health."

"Dancing at the ball will determine the rest of my life, that's why it's more important."

He held in his laugh. Grace looked determined, all jesting gone from her eyes. "I do not understand how dancing could possibly do that."

Grace was amusing in the way she thought about things, and he liked hearing her opinions. He also enjoyed dancing, in fact it was one of the things he'd missed most over the last few years.

"I have it on very good authority that the Duke of Norfolk likes to dance," Grace said.

Warning flags raised in his mind. He kept his breathing slow, unwilling to give anything away. "And why should that matter?"

"It matters because I am a superior dancer. Superior dancers look for superior partners."

He laughs. "I do not think the duke attends balls regularly."

"I have it on good authority that he will be at the Christmas ball. My cousin was quite positive about it. And I must be able to dance by then." She glared at her ankle, as if that would instantly heal her.

"So that he will see you dance?"

"Yes, and so he will fall in love with me."

Oliver laughed again. He couldn't help himself. This conversation was utterly ridiculous to have with a woman in the woods. "Do all women think that men are so easily captured by such skills?"

She shrugged her shoulders nonchalantly, but there was a flash of hurt in her eyes. "I wear the clothes of someone who hasn't fallen on hard times. My family relations are very well off. Why shouldn't dancing lead to marriage?"

"Why should it?" he countered back.

"Because it's one of the best ways to capture someone's attention. A few smiles while we dance, a few flirtatious words, and once I have his attention, we will talk more, and I will win him over so he will fall in love with me."

"He's a gentleman and a widower. I doubt he wants to be looked at as a prize."

"Just as women are looked at as a prize?" She leaned back on the settee.

"Touché. But why is dancing your only option to gain a man's attention?" he asked.

"It is what I am best at. I am not a great beauty, nor overly clever or well-connected. Being a skilled dancer is the only way I can think of to stand out in a room full of beauty."

His breath hitched. He did not agree with Grace's assessment of herself. She was, in fact, very beautiful. And spirited. She was clever and witty, holding her own each time they verbally sparred. Before he could voice any of these thoughts, however, she continued.

"I believe I could make him happy again."

He squinted at her. What game was she playing? "You don't know the first thing about him, aside from a rumor from your cousin that he may or may not come to the Christmas ball."

"That is true. But I am fully aware of my future if I fail to win his attentions." She shuddered. "And I don't like the alternative."

He leaned forward in his chair, more attentive than he had been a moment ago. "What do you mean the alternative?"

"It is nothing," she said, waving her hand in the air.

"I don't believe you," he said, watching her closely.

She glanced around the room before her light brown eyes landed on his. "Are you very good at keeping secrets, Ollie?" she asked, biting her lip between her teeth.

He nodded slowly, wondering what she would say next.

"I have agreed to a marriage of convenience this spring, if I do not secure a match before then. That is why I must dance."

"To find a man to marry," he said slowly.

"Not just anyone. Someone who will be more ... financially ... sound than the current offer I have." She covered her face with her hands. "It sounds truly dreadful when I say it aloud. I know it does, but it is what I need to do."

Oliver schooled his features into the mask that he wore when he was at school, the one that would make others try to guess his own thoughts. "What is so dreadful about the match you have already secured? I did not know that women were in the habit of securing such arrangements, only to get out of them. You want a title, is that it?"

"The arrangement I have right now has a title attached to it. But the earl is twenty years my senior with children already of his own that are nearly as old as I am."

"If the idea is so repulsive to you, I wonder that you tried to secure it." He shook his head. Women, it seemed, were all the same. All trying to get the best situation. A title, a fortune, a parcel of land.

"It is not for me," she said earnestly. "Originally when Papa asked for my help, I thought he only wanted to use my dowry for my younger sisters. After all, I have no prospects, and so I told him he could use it for my twin sisters just younger than me. Both of them will have a London Season this year, and though my relatives are sponsoring them, it is not quite enough."

"So they took your dowry?" he asked.

She shook her head. "Papa said that was not necessary, and that the earl's offer would be something to consider."

"But against your own will?"

She sat up straighter, her eyes flashing. "It is not *against* my will. I *want* to help my family. And this situation gives me a way to do that. I am the eldest. It falls to me to help where I can."

He crossed his arms across his chest. "So you will give up the happiness of a marriage because you want to help your family?"

She lifted one shoulder. "I hope to still find happiness. I

do not plan to give up the idea entirely. And I have a chance to choose at the house party. If there is a situation that would help my family more than what I have now ... that is what I will do. I'd much rather marry someone closer to my own age," she said wistfully, then sighed.

"With such plans, I'm surprised you aren't concerned other guests won't have the same idea. Your cousins for example. Are they not close to your same age?"

"They are a few years younger than me, but I doubt there is a prospect there. My cousin who is married is a neighbor to the duke. She's never said anything about her younger sisters having any interest. I have only just recently decided on the duke, though my cousin has mentioned him before. But other guests are a concern, especially if I cannot dance properly." She glared down at the blanket that was covering her injured ankle.

"What do your cousins get out of sponsoring you in this lunacy?"

She shrugged. "Likely the prestige of being related to the duke's new bride, I'd imagine. And it would set my sisters up for a path where they would be able to marry for love." She leaned back in her chair and sighed again. "How would that be?"

He removed his eyes from her and looked toward the crackling fire, unfocused as the flames danced in the hearth. "It would be the most wonderful thing in the world."

She leaned forward, then winced, trying to straighten her leg on the settee.

Oliver stood and helped adjust the pillow for her under her ankle.

"Thank you," she said softly.

He nodded and returned to his chair, his mind racing around everything Grace had revealed about herself and her situation.

"Do you truly think marrying for love would be the most wonderful thing in the world? It sounds as if you know what it is like to be in love."

He nodded, there was no use denying it. "I have been in love before. Just once." His heart squeezed at the admission.

Grace's eyes grew wider. "What happened?"

"She got away," he said.

"She got away?" she asked, repeating his words.

He shook his head. "It's not important."

Grace's eyes softened, looking at him for a long while, as if trying to figure him out. When she spoke again, her voice was quieter. "I am sorry to hear it."

He swallowed. "Love is worth the heartache. In many ways they go together. Heartache has a way of filling in when love is lost."

"I once wished I would be able to marry for love."

"Then why not pursue it?" He looked at her, pushing away the pity he felt from her gaze.

"I've already told you about my family situation. My parents only have daughters. As the eldest, it is my duty to do what I can to secure their future comforts and happiness. Marriage for me is a transactional arrangement so that my sisters may have a better situation than I have been blessed with."

"That is very noble of you to sacrifice for your family in such a way."

"It is not a sacrifice when you love someone. It may not be the most desirable, but I am willing to do this for my sisters." She looked down at her ankle, sadness in her eyes. "That is why the ankle is so bothersome right now. Such rotten timing, and if it does not heal, I shall never have the opportunity to impress the duke."

He straightened at her words. For all of Society's rules, there was truth to them, and he hated that. "You think he only cares about dancing? Such a shallow thing to think."

"It is not that I think so shallowly of *him*, sir. It is the very fact that to attract attention one must stand out among others. But how can I stand out when I cannot even stand?"

He pressed his lips together, holding in a laugh at her wit.

"Do not laugh at me. It is not a laughing matter." She glared at him, completely helpless as she sat on the settee and huffed.

And then he did laugh. Grace was refreshing, and he couldn't help himself. The laugh filled his lungs and his soul. When he recovered himself, he dared look into her glaring eyes again. "I beg your pardon, Grace, but it was quite funny. Your pun about standing out and standing was quite witty. You'll have to say something equally amusing to the duke."

She shook her head. "I doubt it would impress the duke."

"How would you know? You don't even know him."

"You're right. I don't know him." Her shoulders slumped slightly. "I was hoping to spend time with my cousins asking them all sorts of questions about him. That is why I wanted to arrive before the rest of the guests. But now I doubt there will be much opportunity to discuss the matter."

He laughed again. She was charming. "What do you wish to know of him?"

She raised her eyebrows, an unspoken look of hope filling her eyes. "Do you know him? And you have been keeping such a secret from me?"

He knew it was a bad idea to reveal anything, but she was intriguing, and the way she spoke to a complete stranger about her plans for ensnaring a husband he ought to take care. "Shouldn't you be concerned that if I know him, I will tell him of your scheme?"

She bit her lip. "I shouldn't fear something from you," she said, her voice filled with genuine warmth. "You said we are friends, and that you would do anything to help me."

"The help was in regard to your ankle and healing," he reminded her.

She looked him straight in the eyes, the question boring into him before she voiced it. "Are you going to tell the duke of my plans?"

"*Tell* him?" He glanced around the room. He was walking a very dangerous line. His eyes met hers again, and he noticed the crease between her brows. "No, I will not tell him. As you said, we are friends. I will not speak any of the words you've spoken to me."

The crease between her brows disappeared, a smile of relief forming on her beautiful pink lips. "Thank you, Ollie. You are a true friend."

He nodded. "Considering the circumstance upon which we've met, I do not think I would have credibility if I shared such personal matters with anyone, especially since revealing such secrets could create an even deeper problem."

"What is that?"

"Why, that you were alone with me in my cottage for more than a day, unchaperoned. With such gossip traveling about, I would be forced to marry you to save your reputation, and we wouldn't want that, would we?" He laughed at the joke between them. But as soon as the words were out of his mouth, he held his breath. The answer to the question was suddenly very important.

She colored, her cheeks turning into the hue of crimson roses budding against the white snow in the spring time. "I suppose it is a good thing you have already known what it is to love. I doubt you would be the kind of man who would be caught in such an arrangement."

He studied her for a moment. "I have been in love before, it is true. And I haven't thought about being in love ever again." At least that had been true earlier in the week. Now—now he wasn't so sure. He cleared his throat. "But love or not, no one truly wants to be coerced into the situation of marriage, do they?"

"I suppose no one does. And now you can see my point about wanting to choose who I will marry," she said.

He laughed. "Yes, but in so doing, do you want the duke to have the same choice?"

"Of course I would. I am not trying to trap or ensnare him. I wouldn't trick him into marrying me," she said, her nose raised in the air.

He nodded but didn't respond.

"Would you ever like to marry? So you don't live here all alone?" she asked.

He knew the question was a harmless one, but it was not without difficulty. He schooled his features, letting the mask fall on him like a comfortable cloak. Grace did not need to know that this was a hard question for him.

He brushed off an imaginary piece of lint from his jacket, as if the question meant nothing. "If I ever marry, it will be because I have given my heart to someone, and the only way to ensure the safekeeping of my heart would be to keep the woman by my side forever." He held her gaze, feeling strength in his answer. He hadn't known what he thought until he spoke the words, but he wouldn't take them back. He knew they were true.

She swallowed, then looked at her hands as they smoothed the blanket over her lap. "Your future wife will be lucky to have such a doting husband. What must that be like?"

"I think that's how you know you're living," he said softly, his gaze back on the hearth.

"It sounds like a fairytale, like one of those poems you read."

"A fairytale. Exactly." He jumped from his seat, wanting to pace the room back and forth, but with a guest here, he knew he couldn't. "Shall I prepare tea for you?"

"I should like that. Thank you, Ollie."

He was coming to love the sound of his name on her lips. He unstuck his tongue from the roof of his mouth. "You're welcome, Grace," he replied. Then he retreated to the small kitchen and took his time preparing the tea things. He told himself it was because he needed a little bit of space from this conversation, and not because he wanted everything to look perfect for his guest. He almost convinced himself.

CHAPTER EIGHT

Grace sat on the settee, listening to the clanking of saucers and cups as she sat helplessly by the fire. For a moment she considered following Ollie into the kitchen, using her crutch, but then decided against it. Something had shifted between her and Ollie, and somehow she felt it best to wait where she was. She made a small clicking sound with her tongue, and Apollo's head moved in her direction, ears perked.

"Come here, Apollo."

The dog obeyed, coming close to Grace. She patted his head, and his tail wagged.

"You're a good boy, aren't you? Yes, you are, and not a wolf after all," she said to the dog.

Apollo laid his head in Grace's lap, his eyes expressive. Grace rubbed the top of his head, not fully able to reach down the entirety of the dog's body from where she sat. The dog's eyes closed as she scratched between his ears, stroking his soft fur.

"Apollo is not a lap dog," Ollie said when he came back into the room with the tray.

Grace looked at Ollie, and seeing his smile knew that he wasn't displeased with her attention to the animal. "And he is not sitting on my lap like a small dog."

Ollie grunted. "You'll spoil him."

"I doubt that, I've seen you give him a lot of attention," she said. She scratched behind his ears again, and Apollo closed his eyes. "Who's a good puppy? Yes, you are, Apollo. A very good dog."

Apollo laid his head back in Grace's lap.

Ollie poured her a cup of tea, not asking how she liked it, just remembering how she took it. He held out the cup and saucer to her, and she scratched Apollo's head once more before patting it gently, and then accepting the drink.

"Apollo, come. Let Grace drink her tea," Ollie said, as he poured his own cup.

Apollo didn't move.

Grace willed herself not to laugh at Ollie's frustration as the dog was content with her. She took another sip of her tea, pretending to ignore Ollie's continual commanding to the dog. Finally, she looked at the dog in the eyes, patted him on the head again, and said, "Apollo, Ollie could use some attention." She pointed to where Ollie sat in his chair, and the dog wagged his tail and went to his master.

Ollie scowled at Apollo. "Traitor."

At that Grace laughed, nearly spilling her tea. "Oh, he is no such thing. I think he's very loyal, aren't you, Apollo? Such a good boy."

The dog wagged his tail, his tongue lopping out of his mouth at the praise from Grace.

Grace smiled triumphantly.

Ollie shook his head and patted his dog.

Grace stirred her tea with a spoon. "Now that I know that you will keep my secret, will you tell me about the duke?"

Ollie's eyes changed. She'd seen this happen several times since she had arrived. At first, she couldn't name it, but now, it looked like he was being guarded. His square jaw worked back and forth, probably in an unconscious manner, and Grace wondered about that. It was not as if she were a threat, was she? After all, she had no intention of telling anyone about their time together either. Their mutual secret was safe.

He smiled, but his smile didn't quite reach his eyes the way it had when he'd been laughing and sharing a joke with her. "What would you like to know? I will see if I can be useful, though I cannot answer all questions about him."

She hadn't expected him to answer all of her questions. She didn't think he could truly know the duke that well. And that gave her pause. What if Ollie didn't know the duke? Or he was teasing her for his own amusement? She tamped down her momentary doubts. "How old is he?"

He raised an eyebrow. "Surely you know this already."

She swallowed. "I want to know that I can trust your information." And she needed to go back and reread her cousin's letters, but most of them were back in her trunks. Her cousin had always sent news of the people in her town. Surely, she could have just waited until she'd gotten to her cousin's house.

Ollie smiled knowingly. "He's twenty-nine. How old are you?"

She raised her eyebrow. "I thought you said you weren't going to tell him anything about me."

"I shall not tell him that we've spoken. We've already established how terrible it would be for both of us if we were forced to marry one another." He raised his eyebrows.

She swallowed. It was the forced to marry part that she had a problem with, and the scandal that such an arrangement would spread ... but, time together with Ollie wasn't unenjoyable. She blinked, unwilling to verbalize or think further on that. "Then why should you like to know my age?"

He leaned back in his chair, looking completely at ease. His manner was always easy, as if he didn't have a care in the world. As if everything about this cottage made him content. She envied that carefree attitude.

"I should like to have a *conversation* with you, Grace. Only answering questions makes me feel like I am being accused of a crime. You said I have no tact in the way I treat the fairer sex, and so I am practicing. Help me by answering a question for each one you ask."

She looked at him thoughtfully. There was a light in his eyes, and she quite liked that. And she could help him practice conversing while she was in his house. Perhaps one day he would meet someone he fancied, and this time of practicing, as he called it, would suit him. "I suppose there is not harm in helping a friend. Very well, I accept your terms. I am twenty-three years old."

He raised his eyebrow. "You do not look twenty-three," he said matter-of-factly.

She shook her head, a laugh escaping. "These are precisely the kind of statements that you should not say to a woman. Asking her age is impertinent enough."

"So it is not impertinent if a woman asks about age, but it is when a man does?" he challenged.

She laughed. "Oh it's impertinent both ways, but I'm not asking *your* age, or commenting on how you don't look that age. I'm asking the duke's age."

He laughed. "Ah, now I see the difference."

She bit her lip, curiosity niggling into her. It shouldn't matter what Ollie thought. It didn't. But still, the question was out of her mouth before she could stop it. "Do I look older or younger than twenty-three, in your opinion?"

He smiled, the warmth from his look filling her like a cup of perfectly brewed hot tea. "That depends. For which answer will I get in less trouble?" His eyes danced with mirth.

She rolled her eyes and threw a small pillow at him. It

missed him, and Apollo looked toward her, ears perked. "You are very incorrigible."

"I think my governess would agree with you."

"You had a governess?" Somehow, she had not considered that before. Not that she had thought much about Ollie's growing up years.

"Why is that surprising?"

It felt as though tea was stuck in her throat. "It's not, it's just ... I hadn't thought ... considering your home." She gestured around. "I am sorry. I didn't mean to offend. I did not mean to sound surprised."

OLIVER STUDIED GRACE. SHE WAS VERY PRETTY WHEN she was flustered. Somehow the perfect poise and grace she possessed was ruffled, and he liked it. He was not offended by her words. On the contrary, she wouldn't have been far from the mark, if this had been his true home. No one would have considered someone living in such humble circumstances to have had a governess. Perhaps it was good to keep her guessing about himself, while she was interested in the duke.

"I am not offended at all," he said, smiling.

She nodded. "Thank you for your generosity."

He could tell that there was still an awkwardness around her, but he wasn't ready to stop talking for the evening. He was playing a dangerous game, but a few more questions wouldn't hurt, would they? Not if he was able to learn about her in the process.

"How old do you think I am?" he asked, going back to their earlier question.

She pressed her lips together as if keeping in a secret. "I do not think it would be wise to guess. At any rate, I shall not be able to say with any certainty. I do not think you are twenty years my senior," she said, laughter returning into her eyes at the jest.

He smiled. "You are right on at least that account. I am twenty-nine."

"The same age as the duke," she said.

He nodded, unwilling to say those same words back.

She tapped her chin, as if thinking hard about a puzzle. "Ah, that's how you know about him. You must have been at the same schools growing up?"

He spoke slowly, measuring each word. "We attended the same schools."

"And are the rumors true? Does he like dancing? Would dancing be a way into his heart?"

He took the question, and looked for a way to be objective about the topic. Would it be? "I believe it would be a way to gain his favor, yes. The duke is notorious for his superior dancing, as you already know."

"And you've known him a long time?" she pressed.

He swallowed. He wouldn't lie. He would never lie to Grace. "I cannot remember a time when I didn't know him."

She nodded. "And was his ... wife ... a good dancer?"

The cup and saucer trembled in his hand. He took a quick sip of tea, then set the cup and saucer onto the table. "That is not a question about the duke."

Her eyes widened. "You're right. It's not. I … I am sorry. It was not appropriate to pry. Besides, she must have been a good dancer. I imagine she would have been."

He took a long breath, wishing there was somewhere for the pain to go. "She was the most beautiful dancer."

"What happened to her, if you don't mind my asking," she said softly.

"Are you testing me again? You likely know what happened."

She shook her head, sincerity in her features. "I do not. I have never asked about it. It feels irreverent to ask about it."

"But you're asking a stranger in the woods."

"We're friends, Ollie, not strangers," she said with determination.

He swallowed. "A riding accident. Horse threw her, and she hit a tree." He kept his voice even, neutral. "The duke tried to help her, but there was nothing he could do. She was gone before the doctors arrived."

Grace gasped, her hand covering her throat. "That's dreadful."

He only nodded. Dreadful. Terrible. Tragic. Those were words that didn't even come close to describing the horror. He took a sip of his tea, and took a small bite of the bread.

"It's your turn to ask me a question now," she said.

He gave her a small smile. "I do not think I can think of any more questions tonight."

She nodded, her eyes sad. "I am sorry I upset you. I didn't mean to upset you."

The air between them felt heavy. "You didn't upset me. But retelling her story made me think how panicked I was when I found a woman alone in the forest two days ago. When I think of what happened to the duke's wife ..." He swallowed the rest of the sentence. Emotion rose in his throat, and he stood in front of her, his words clawing. "Something very dangerous could have happened to you. You were foolish for riding away from the safety of your party."

Her eyes seemed to spark at his words. "Foolish? From my understanding, it was half a day's ride on a good road." Her voice was full of challenge.

He narrowed his eyes, his pulse racing. "You could have been seriously hurt. Or worse."

She straightened, her voice rising. "Thankfully, I wasn't and I *am* healing, as you see."

Anger rose inside of him at her lack of understanding. Could she not see the error of her ways? Suddenly his lodge felt too confined, the space between them too tense. "I'm going to feed the horses," he said, not waiting for an answer before he stormed from the lodge and into the storm without his great coat.

He took his time in the stable, using the full length of the building to pace back and forth after feeding the horses.

Finally, he returned to his hunting lodge. Opening the front door, he saw Grace staring toward the window. Two steps into the room, their gazes locked on each other.

"I am sorry I shouted," Grace said, her words rapidly tumbling out. "I should not have done such a thing. It was most uncalled for."

He crossed the distance between them, coming to stand close to her. Then on an impulse he knelt down in front of her. "I am sorry that I called you foolish."

She put a hand on his arm, her eyes shining as she shook her head. Her lips trembled as she spoke. "You are right. I was foolish. And I'm sorry. You have no idea how sorry I am for that choice."

He glanced toward the blanket where her ankle was elevated with a pillow. "Because now you won't be able to dance and impress the duke, I know."

Her eyes widened, then her lashes fluttered rapidly. "That's not it at all. I'm sorry for the situation I'm in and for the situation I've put you in. I'm sorry that you are sleeping on this settee while I commandeer your room. I've been a burden on you. I've been a burden on my family. And yes, that means I'm sorry that my ankle is in such a state because I had hoped to get myself *out* of this situation. Instead I've just made everything worse." A few tears streaked down each of her cheeks, falling off when they reached her jawline.

His heart swelled. "Don't cry," he said softly.

"I'm not crying," she said with fire as she wiped away

the evidence of tears from her cheeks. She turned away from him. "I know I was foolish. And though I'm sorry for all of the trouble I've been for you, I'm grateful you saved me. And you chased after my wild horse. I am indebted to you. Thank you."

Her hand moved down from where she'd been holding his arm, sliding until her ungloved fingers touched his. She took his hand in both of hers and then kissed the back of his hand. A tear fell onto one of his knuckles, as if to quell the fire that had roared to life in the spot where she'd kissed him.

"I am glad that you are safe," he said, taking his hand from hers and wiping away a few of her tears with his thumb. Her skin was soft to his touch. His fingers cradled her soft jawline for only a moment, and he convinced himself that wiping away a few more tears was an excuse. "Do not cry. You are safe now."

She took a deep breath. "Thank you, Ollie."

"Allow me to help you to your room."

She nodded, and he gave her the crutch and helped her to stand. He stayed close to her, offering his support to her as he escorted her to the room. He helped her to the chair where her other dress lay so she could change for bed.

"I will be just outside if you need anything," he said, before closing the door behind her.

CHAPTER NINE

Grace sat looking at the glass and composed herself. She wasn't consumed by her appearance, generally, but with her hair a mess, and her eyes swollen from the tears, she needed more than a little time in front of the glass. She took a small towel and dipped it into the basin, cleaning her face and hands.

Her neck still showed the residual white and red splotches from the emotion she'd let spill from her eyes, but at least her cheeks were starting to return to their normal state. She combed her hair quickly, determined to braid it and make it look more decent than it was.

The look in Ollie's eyes when he'd told her what happened to the duke's wife had shown real fear there. She'd seen it. Had he been concerned for her life like that? He had saved her life, and she would be eternally grateful for his act of heroism. He was the bravest, kindest man she'd ever had the privilege of meeting. Even now, he was sheltering her while the storm continued, day in and day out. She dabbed at her eyes once more, determined to remove the redness and make herself look more presentable.

When she was ready for bed, she surveyed the room. Ollie had been so generous to give up his room the past two nights, but with a renewed vigor, she positioned her crutch underneath her arm and hopped toward the door. She leaned against the wall, balancing as she held her crutch and tried to open the door.

But it gave way too easily and Ollie was on the other side of the door. His eyes softened when they took her in. "Grace, what are you doing?" he asked. "I can fetch you anything you need."

"I am glad to hear it because there is something I need," she said matter-of-factly, heading directly for the settee. Her progress was slow by herself.

He followed next to her. "Allow me to assist you," he said. He helped her to the settee, then sat beside her. He laid her crutch at her feet and asked, "How can I help?"

"I should like to make the settee my bed tonight. Could you bring me an extra blanket?" She smiled up at him.

"That is not necessary, Grace. The bed is much more comfortable than this settee."

"Exactly. You are much taller than I am. I imagine you cannot stretch out at all on this settee. Besides now that I am out here, I do not believe I should attempt walking back to the bedroom." She glanced at her foot, surprised at just how sore it felt from the small distance.

"I could always carry you," he said, lifting an eyebrow.

Her cheeks warmed at the idea. "Then what would become of this beautiful walking stick you made me? I should hate for it to go to waste."

"I do not like the idea of making a guest sleep on a settee. It is unheard of."

She laughed. It was such an absurd thing for him to say. "Next time you rescue a woman in the woods, you can make that a condition. But for now, I'm quite content to sleep out here. Besides, Apollo shall keep me company."

He studied her for a moment. "I can see you are not going to change your mind easily on this subject."

"Not at all," she said firmly.

He nodded once. "Very well. I shall bring you extra blankets and a pillow on one condition."

"What is that?"

"That you let me know if it is too uncomfortable for you to sleep out here."

"It will be comfortable enough."

"You will tell me if it isn't?" He eyed her, waiting for her to agree with him.

She nodded. "Very well. I will."

He stood, then went into the other room. He came back with an armful of blankets and a pillow. He helped arrange everything, making the settee look like a bed.

She slipped between the covers, pulling up the blankets

to her neck. "How did you manage to sleep on this? I fit very well, but I cannot imagine you were comfortable at all."

He smiled at her. "I made do. And I would make do again, if need be," he said. "I brought the book out with me, in case you would like to continue our story hour." Then something crossed his face. "Of course, I understand if you do not wish to."

She noticed the small red-leather volume on the small table that he referred to. "I would enjoy that very much," she said, closing her eyes though she wanted to watch his expressions as he read. She felt a furry face on her middle and opened her eyes just slightly to see Apollo next to her, and Ollie scowling at the dog. She rubbed the top of his head and Ollie began reading again. His voice was soothing, the timbre rich and vibrant. With each sonnet he read, she relaxed a little more as she allowed his voice to carry her into sleep.

GRACE AWOKE WITH A START. BLINKING IN THE darkness she tried to make sense of what she'd heard. She was disoriented until she remembered she'd insisted upon sleeping on the settee. The wind blew outside, but that had not caused her to stir since her first night coming to the cottage. She sat up when she heard the noise again. Apollo's whimper came from somewhere in the darkness. Reaching behind her she found the small candle perched there, and lit the wick. It didn't illuminate much in the room, but Apollo wasn't next to her. She held the candle aloft when she heard the sound again. A terrified moaning, followed by Apollo's whimper in the far corner of the room.

Heart pounding, she put the candle back on the table and reached for her crutch. After some maneuvering she was out of the covers and leaning heavily on the crutch as she made her way to Ollie's bedroom.

Apollo's whimpers increased as Grace approached. "It's alright, Apollo," she whispered soothingly.

Another moan from behind the door came, and she knew immediately that things were not alright. Without knocking, Grace opened the door, and Apollo immediately bounded into the room.

"Ollie. It is me Grace," she said, announcing her presence. Apollo continued to whimper, and Grace moved farther into the room. "Are you hurt?"

He didn't answer.

Her eyes adjusted to the blackness, but she wished she'd brought the candle from the other room. She bumped into a chair but was able to catch herself from falling. She felt around the dressing table, and found a small candle, and lit it quickly.

She held up the candle and saw Ollie shaking, his face covered in beads of sweat, his eyes shut tightly.

Grace moved quickly toward the bed, pushing through the pain as she moved with the crutch. She gripped the candle holder tightly, putting it on the small side table before gently touching Ollie's shoulder. "Ollie. You must wake up. You are safe in your own home and in your own bed. You are having a bad dream."

Ollie's eyes flew open wildly. He sat straight up, his breathing ragged. Apollo barked and the sound seemed to snap Ollie out of the moment.

"You are going to be all right," Grace said soothingly. "You are safe inside from whatever happened in your nightmare. I'm here to help you." Grace said it as the reason why she was in his room in the middle of the night.

His face was as white as his sheets, his shirtsleeves drenched in sweat. He blinked hard, then finally let out a deep sigh.

Grace let out the breath she had been holding. He was coming out of the dream, coming back to reality. She could see it. "Shall I bring you a glass of water?" she asked.

He shook his head. He looked haggard.

Grace didn't want to overstep her boundaries, but she knew from experience that Ollie probably couldn't make the best decisions at the moment. She went to his wardrobe and pulled out a clean shirt. She handed it to him, then turned around. "You should change out of the shirt you are in. You do not want to catch a chill." She waited until she heard the movement of him changing.

"I have changed," he said, his voice tired.

She turned around and took a tentative step closer. "Would you like to talk about it?"

"No."

Grace studied him for a moment. "Apollo, up," she said, patting the foot of the bed.

"My dog doesn't sleep on my bed," Ollie said, just as Apollo obeyed Grace, and laid on his master's feet, looking up at him.

"I think Apollo will feel much better tonight if he can stay in here with you. He was whimpering at your door for quite some time."

Lines extended on his forehead and between his brows. "I am sorry he disturbed you."

Grace didn't respond to that. In truth, it wasn't Apollo that she'd heard to begin with. No one need apologize for having a nightmare—it was not something that could be controlled. Though there was usually some sort of trigger to them, she couldn't think what it might be since she didn't understand the situation. But speaking the truth might lead the conversation toward Grace prying for more information. And he'd already made it clear that he didn't want to discuss it. She left it alone to ponder later.

Instead, she picked up the book still on the table beside the bed. "Shall I read to you from this *very* fascinating book about native plants?"

"You think it's fascinating now?"

She smiled. "Oh it's riveting. Just the thing to put one to sleep."

"I enjoy the book, thank you very much."

Grace smiled at his words. His old humor seemed to come through. He was likely going to be alright, but she wanted to make sure for herself. "Then I shall read it for you." She sat in the same chair that he'd occupied on the previous nights he'd read to her. She'd had enough of the introduction, so she let the book fall open to somewhere in the middle. Turning a few pages, she found the beginning of a chapter, marked with a large number four and a decorated letter T. "*The study of plants in their native land is a subject not to be discarded. Each unique plant is connected to those around it and therefore, deserves attention from both a general and a specific look of the area.*"

Grace continued reading the book, glancing up every few sentences to survey Ollie. His features were more relaxed, and his eyes were closed. She knew from experience that it could take a long time to recover from a nightmare, but she hoped that the familiarity of the words in this book would help soothe him. She read for nearly an hour until she could hear the shift in his breathing from shallow to deeper. She closed the book and rested it on her lap, caressing the spine as she watched Ollie for a while longer, sending up a silent prayer that he would be able to sleep comfortably for the rest of the night.

Apollo lifted his head when Grace stood up. She patted the dog's head, rubbing behind his ears. "Take care of your master tonight, Apollo," she whispered.

She looked back toward Ollie. He was sleeping now. She carefully lifted the covers over him, brushing aside the hair that fell over his brow. She pulled her hand back and her breathing raced. Touching Ollie while he was sleeping in his shirtsleeves was highly improper. She rubbed at where her fingers had made contact with his skin, but the tingling sensation still remained.

He stirred, and she stepped away from him, settling back into the chair and opening the botany book. She would read to him for a little longer just to make sure that he didn't have a repeat episode. Angling the book toward the short candle, she found her place, and continued to read about native flowers in the area.

CHAPTER TEN

Oliver's head was heavy when he awoke the next morning. Something shifted at his feet. His dog, Apollo, was at the end of his bed, covering his feet. Memories of the evening drifted back to him. Apollo was never allowed on his bed. But Grace had given him permission.

He looked over to the chair in his room, his eyes landing on Grace slumped in the chair. She was a rare woman. She'd stopped the terror that had infected his dreams the night before. Suddenly the events of last night came running back to him, feeling like a blow. The nightmare was a terrible one, the thought of it now sent prickles down his spine. He pushed the thoughts away, when he looked at Grace. She'd helped him. She'd pulled him out of the abyss. His heart warmed at the thought. She was safe. His nightmare wasn't a reality, it had all been just a dream.

She was still sleeping soundly, still holding onto the book she'd read from last night. Her voice had a melodic quality to it, calming him and counteracting the images that lurked beneath the surface of his dreams.

He swung his feet off the bed, standing slowly. Apollo moved his head, then settled back into the covers. Grace hadn't moved. He quietly took a blanket and put it around her. He didn't want to disturb her sleep. "Thank you, Grace," he barely whispered.

A small curl was in front of her face, and he gently tucked it behind her ear. Her skin was smooth, her ringlet soft. He pulled his fingers back, heat searing from where he'd made contact with the side of her temple.

He stepped back and quickly grabbed his clothes so he could change in the other room. With a few soft pats to his thigh, Apollo jumped down from the bed and followed him out of the bedroom. He headed outside to take care of the horses, then brought in an armload of firewood on his way back into the house.

GRACE AWOKE IN THE CHAIR. SHE BLINKED. HAD SHE fallen asleep while watching over Ollie? Her stiff neck protested as she looked up to where Ollie was, only to find that the bed was vacant. How had she fallen asleep while attending to someone? She couldn't remember ever doing that when she kept vigil over her sister after a nightmarish episode. Rubbing her sore neck, she reached down for her crutch. She moved toward the open bedroom door but couldn't see Ollie in the room beyond. She closed the door just to be certain and changed back into her only other option of dresses. Sitting in front of the glass, she made quick work of her hair. She wasn't overly skilled at creating elegance with her hair, but today she wanted to do something more than a simple, long braid down her back. Her hair pins were in a small pile next to her mother's comb, and she used them to secure a simple chignon. She gave her hair a critical look. It was not expertly done, but it was what she could do without the help of a maid or a sister.

Apollo barked, and Grace picked up her crutch. She'd barely opened the door before Apollo came bounding in toward her. He sat expectantly in front of Grace.

She leaned over and scratched the animal behind his ears and the dog's eyes closed. "Good morning, Apollo."

He stayed by her side as they walked out of the bedroom together.

Ollie stoked the fire in the main living area. He stood and bowed as Grace approached. She dropped into a slight curtsy, but the gesture felt uncomfortable with her crutch. His direct gaze stayed locked on her. She wanted to say something to him, but she wasn't sure how to phrase what she wanted to know. But Ollie broke the silence first.

"I see that you preferred the chair instead of the settee," he said. "I cannot think which one is more uncomfortable."

She smiled. He'd added a lightness to the situation. "I apologize. I meant no slight on your very fine settee."

He stepped toward her, taking her hand in his. "It is I who needs to apologize. I never meant to interrupt your sleep."

A spark of heat fluttered from where his ungloved hand touched her own, sending waves through her arm and up her neck. The pleasant tingling rendered her momentarily speechless. Finally, she said, "One doesn't need to apologize for having a nightmare, Ollie. It is not something one can control."

He brought his other hand on top of hers, sending more thrills along the length of her arm. "Still, I am very grateful for your service to me. And I do apologize you were not comfortable due to a result of my own actions, whether I could control them or not."

"It was not uncomfortable," she said slowly. "And I was happy to help, however I could."

He nodded. "Apollo also gained from the experience. He is not generally allowed on beds. I have a feeling you may have spoiled him."

Grace smiled, then reached down and stroked Apollo's sleek coat. "Perhaps it was my plan all along so that Apollo would like me better."

Ollie chuckled and shook his head. "I do not think you needed to allow him such freedom to gain that. It is clear Apollo shows a preference for you. He listens to you better than he does to me."

"I will remind him to listen to you better," Grace said. She looked down at Apollo. "I believe you should listen to Ollie, Apollo."

The dog panted, wagging his tail at Grace's words.

"Are you hungry for breakfast?" he asked, pulling his hands away.

"Yes," she said, immediately missing the warmth of his touch.

He nodded. "I will start preparing it," he said, walking toward the kitchen.

Grace's heart pounded. "Could I be of use in the kitchen? There is no need to wait on me in such a manner. I can get around with the crutch."

He nodded. "Of course you are welcome to help. But I also do not mind waiting on you."

She could feel her cheeks heating as he looked at her. She swallowed. "I should like to help," she said finally.

As it turned out breakfast was not something Grace could easily help with. Warming the toast and preparing the eggs required two hands and no crutch. Instead Grace sat on a stool and cut the bread.

Grace had wanted to continue talking with Ollie, but he started whistling the moment he began making breakfast. She listened to the tune, a happy boisterous one she couldn't name. When he finished one of his refrains, she clapped. "I enjoy that tune. What is it?"

He grinned. "I do not actually know. It is one that Cook

used to hum." He paused, his eyes wide. "I used to spend a lot of time in the stairwell of the kitchen."

"You did? Whatever for?"

"To steal the hottest biscuits and sweet breads of course."

Grace laughed. "I do not believe it."

"It's true. There came a point in the melody when I knew that Cook would be finished. Then she'd stop whistling for a moment, say something to the others in the kitchen, and then go back to whistling. I always knew I had about ten seconds to carefully lift one of the rolls or cakes from the tray. They were conveniently located on the edge of the counter, and I could reach them without being spotted if I was very careful."

"Did anyone ever catch you?"

He shook his head. "Of course not. I was too stealthy," he said confidently. "Though there was this one time ..." He let the sentence dangle for a moment.

Grace eyed him, waiting for him to go on. When he didn't, she prodded, "What happened?"

"One time, I was coming down the stairs, about to perch at my post as usual, when one of the kitchen maids came up the stairs. She asked what I was doing."

"What did you tell her?"

"That the cooking was so delicious I wanted to learn how to make scones."

Grace laughed, picturing in her mind's eye a small boy

with bright blue eyes pretending to fool the kitchen maid. It made for an adorable picture. "Did it work?"

Ollie laughed. "Of course it did. She brought me to the cook, explained what I wanted to know, and Cook showed me how to make scones."

"And you were never caught for stealing the cakes?"

"I never had to steal them when Cook explained that one of the duties of a true cook is to ensure that the food taste delicious for those eating it."

"And how does one do that without any experience?" Grace asked.

"Why, by trying all of the creations," Ollie said triumphantly, pulling out scones from the stove.

"You were very clever as a boy."

"Or hungry."

"You seem to be in a very good humor, considering—" She stopped herself. Why had she tried to bring the conversation back to last night again.

"Considering what?" he asked, his eyes searching hers.

She dropped her eyes to her plate, focusing on the swirls of steam coming up from her scone. "It is nothing."

His face seemed to fill with understanding. "Considering my emotional state from last night," he finished, a grim look on his face.

"I apologize. I do not mean to pry. My sister has had several episodes of nightmares, and sometimes it takes her days before she is feeling like herself again."

"Your sister suffers from nightmares?"

Grace nodded. "Since she was a little girl."

His eyes held warmth. "Then I am indeed sad for her. They can be terrible things."

"Have you always had them?" she asked.

He shook his head. "They are a more recent development in my life," he said solemnly.

"Are they always the same?" she asked him.

He nodded slowly. "More or less they are about the same things."

"My sister has similar patterns. Though, she has found that when she shares the dreams in the daylight she is less frightened by them."

"Do they stop her nightmares?"

Grace shook her head. "Not entirely. But she rarely has a repeat of the same dream."

Ollie held up the prepared plates of food and brought them to the small dining table adjacent to the kitchen. "And do you stay up with her all night, too?"

"I take turns with my sisters, but I find that I am usually able to stay awake for the entire night after an episode. Consequently, I take the most turns."

"You are very kind to do it. And do you read to her too?"

Grace nodded. "Yes, though I do not have so riveting a book on botany as you possess."

"It works like a charm," he said, smiling at her over his plate of food.

"And sometimes I sing."

"I did not know you sing."

"I do not sing very well. I do not perform well in front of others. I sing because it soothes her, and it's the least I can do."

"You are a woman of many gifts, I see," he said approvingly.

"I do what I can," she said, feeling her cheeks grow warm again at his praise.

"I should enjoy hearing you sing."

"Without a pianoforte?"

"Isn't that how you sing to your sister?"

"I sing to her when she's had a nightmare."

He raised an eyebrow at her admission.

"But singing for others is different."

His lips twitched. "I do not have a pianoforte here."

"Then I am afraid I would not be able to sing well at all." She laughed.

"I very much doubt that," he said, the added, "Shall we play a game of checkers this morning?"

She nodded. He likely didn't play too many games by himself in the woods. She would oblige him again, though she knew that she would be sorely beaten in the game. "That sounds like an excellent idea," she said.

He stood from the table, taking their empty plates. "I will be right back with the set. Apollo, would you like to come with me?"

Apollo lifted his head, then put it back down, content to stay by Grace's side.

Ollie shook his head and left the room, though Grace didn't think he was too put out by his animal's behavior.

OLIVER PLACED THE CHECKER BOARD BETWEEN THE two of them on the table. "Would you like to play with the red pieces or the black?" he asked her, holding up two small velvet bags for Grace to choose.

Grace reached for the bag he held in his left hand. "I believe I shall try my luck with the black pieces this time. I had no luck the other day with the red pieces."

Oliver nodded and they set up their pieces. He retrieved an extra piece from each of their piles, to be used to crown the kings later in the game, and put them back into the velvet bag. He shook the contents then held the bag for Grace to reach into. "Whichever piece you draw will indicate the person who will play first."

She reached her hand inside the small bag and pulled it out again. She smiled when she revealed the black piece in her hand. "It looks like today might be my lucky day," she said, sliding her first piece diagonally into a new square.

With each movement on the board they also took turns asking and answering questions, just as they had the first time they'd played checkers. Oliver enjoyed the questions part of the game more than the game itself.

After the fifth game, Grace groaned. "I have never lost

so badly at checkers in my entire life. How are you good at a game that requires no skill?"

Oliver chuckled. "Clearly it requires some skill."

Grace stuck her lip out, pouting slightly. "I cannot believe that my luck is so bad. I even chose the black ones purposefully because they were so lucky for you the other day."

"It is not luck in this game. It is skill."

She waved her fingers in the air. "Games like archery and billiards require skill. Checkers is simply a game of chance."

"Then clearly *chance* is not on your side today."

"I have never been beaten so thoroughly before. My only comfort is that Apollo is on my side," she said, flashing him a challenging grin while Apollo's head laid in her lap.

He threw one of his pieces in the air, catching it, and repeating the process. "Shall I teach you how to have more luck?"

She crossed her arms. "One cannot teach someone how to gain luck."

He threw another piece in the air, catching it in the palm of his hand before resetting the board. "That is true, but I can teach you how to strategize in this game, and that's essentially the same thing."

CHAPTER ELEVEN

Grace squealed in delight. After an entire afternoon of playing checkers, interrupted only by the occasional cup of tea, she at last won a game of checkers against Ollie. She had a sneaking suspicion that he was going easy on her while he'd been teaching her his strategy, but nevertheless it had worked, and she grinned.

"Well-played," Ollie said, grinning. "Even if it is only a game of luck."

Grace's jaw dropped. "That, sir, was no stroke of luck. It took very careful planning, and quite a bit of coaching to best you."

"And you only fought against my advice half a dozen times during this game, so I also consider that a win."

She laughed. "Touché."

"Would you like to play again?" he asked.

Grace shook her head. "It is too much pressure to repeat another win. I am satisfied that I won the last game."

He smiled. "I can appreciate that strategy."

"Perhaps we could read together instead."

"That sounds like excellent entertainment for after dinner, that is if you will not sing." His eyes looked slightly hopeful.

She bit her lip. "I am afraid that you have built my voice up in your head to be something more than it is."

"I suppose there is only one way to find out for sure," he said.

"And what is that?"

"Singing of course."

She smiled, a nervous anticipation swirling inside her. "I confess, I sing much better when I have an instrument to accompany me," she repeated her earlier reservation.

He nodded with understanding. "I shall not pressure you to sing. Reading sounds like an excellent way to spend the evening, though you will have to put up with my dull voice again."

She laughed. "It is not dull at all."

His eyes locked on hers, forcing the breath out of her. She wasn't sure if she was in the middle of inhaling or exhaling, but she couldn't do either in that moment.

Apollo nuzzled his head against her hand, and the movement seemed to break the clear moment between them.

He cleared his throat. "I will tend to the horses before

we eat," he said. "Come, Apollo."

The dog whimpered only for a moment, but then seeing where Ollie was headed, he bounded along behind him.

She resumed breathing—inhaling and then exhaling—like she'd always done. Something had passed between them —something that had been building. She couldn't put her finger on it precisely, only that she knew she enjoyed bantering with him. They'd spent the entirety of every day together since they'd met in such close quarters, and yet, she'd enjoyed her time with him, and hadn't been tired of his company once.

He was back in the room, sitting next to her again, before she'd registered that he'd even come through the door. Apollo came bounding in beside him, then turned in a circle, tail wagging furiously.

"I have some wonderful news, Grace."

She warmed at the tender way he pronounced her Christian name. "What is it? Apollo, what are you so excited about?"

"The storm has slowed down considerably," he said.

Grace blinked. The curtains had been completely drawn most of the days since she'd arrived to keep the heat in. There was only a small window in the dining room, and it had also been covered. She forced a smile. "That is good news," she said, trying to keep her voice sounding happy. After all, having the storm finally dissipate was a happy thing, was it not?

"Apollo knows he will not be kept indoors for much

longer. He is well behaved, but he has missed his freedom."

"I know how he feels," she said, nodding to her ankle. "I wish I could run outdoors right now too." She patted the dog's head.

"Speaking of, how is your ankle?" he asked, coloring at the word.

Grace smiled. It didn't seem odd for Ollie to ask after her, as he had done so every day since coming to his home. "I believe it gets a little better every day. I have to keep believing that."

He nodded. "That is good to hear. Soon you will be with your cousin, and getting the care of a proper physician. Then you will be able to join in at the house party as planned."

He frowned, and for a moment Grace wondered if he was not enjoying the prospect of her leaving either. But then he looked toward her ankle. "Do you think you'll be comfortable enough to ride?"

Grace's smile faltered. She was not in a hurry to leave the comfort and safety of this cottage, the surrounding woods, or the company of Ollie yet. But she knew since the first day that she wasn't going to stay here forever. Still the thought of leaving left her feeling empty. She mustered up her courage. She didn't want to be a burden to him. And he'd been so generous to let her stay so long. "If you will give me the directions, I shall leave after supper."

Ollie's eyes widened. "There is not enough light for us to begin our journey tonight. We would not arrive until long after nightfall. We will start our journey as soon as we can tomorrow morning, provided the storm has fully abated," he said.

"We?"

"You will not be traveling by yourself," he said with finality.

"I won't?" A shimmer of happiness filled her as she thought about being able to spend more time with him tomorrow. She liked spending time with Ollie. But once she was gone, would she ever see him again? Suddenly the house party, the balls, and even the duke, didn't feel like the right path. What was wrong with a cozy cottage in the woods? Nothing.

"Of course you will not be traveling alone. It was a mistake to be out here alone before, and I will not repeat the mistake by letting you ride off alone." He shuddered. "I wouldn't dream of it."

Warmth spread through her at his words. He was a gentleman, in every sense of the word, wanting to see for himself that she made it to her cousin's estate safely, and that she would receive care from a physician. Grace swallowed. "That is most kind of you."

"I wouldn't hear of anything else," he said in a commanding tone that she had noticed a few times since meeting Ollie. "Besides, there are too many miles for me to explain every twist and turn. I will escort you to your cousin's estate."

Grace nodded. "Shall I help you with dinner

preparations?"

"I always enjoy having your company," he said, holding out his arm to escort her into the kitchen.

THE PREPARATIONS FOR DINNER AND THE MEAL ITSELF went by too quickly for Grace's liking. She tried not to focus on the fact that this was her last evening with Ollie, but the pervasive thought creeped in between each pause in their conversation. Far too soon they finished their meal, and Ollie carried their dishes back into the kitchen.

He came back to escort her from the dining room back to the settee in front of the fire. Excusing himself for a moment he left the room and then came back with a volume tucked in the crook of his arm. It had a picture of a tree and a variety of flowers. Without so much as saying a word to her, he settled into the chair by the fire and began reading about botany in his monotonous tone.

Grace laughed, her mood lightening at his joke. "Are we to spend the evening studying about plants that are covered by snow? Should you wish to hold a class on such things, it would be much more enjoyable to be outside comparing the book with the plants in the area."

"That is an excellent idea. If only it wasn't the middle of winter." He closed the book, then took the red leather volume from its place on the side table. "Perhaps some Shakespeare instead?"

She settled in against the cushions. "I should like that."

He read several sonnets. The timbre of his voice transforming from the dull monotonous tone that he teased her with when he read the book on botany. Each line felt like a melody, each sonnet another song. Grace was swept away into the imagery as he continued to read. Each sonnet was more beautiful than the last, each one capturing her heart in a new way.

Take all my loves, my love, yea, take them all:
What hast thou then more than thou hadst before?
No love, my love, that thou mayst true love call—
All mine was thine before thou hadst this more.
Then if for my love thou my love receivest,
I cannot blame thee for my love thou usest;
But yet be blamed if thou this self deceivest
By wilful taste of what thyself refusest.
I do forgive thy robb'ry, gentle thief,
Although thou steal thee all my poverty;
And yet love knows it is a greater grief
To bear love's wrong than hate's known injury.
Lascivious grace, in whom all ill well shows,
Kill me with spites, yet we must not be foes.

He closed the book, and she sat up straighter. "You cannot finish on that one," she said.

"Why ever not?" he asked, an amused expression on his face.

"The last line speaks of killing. Surely it is not one to leave in the memory."

"It also talks about not being foes." He eyed her than opened up the book. "Shall you choose, or shall I?"

"Turn to a random page," she said.

He did, reading a few more poems about love and warriors and dancing.

Grace sighed at the word dance.

Ollie looked up. "What is it? Is your ankle in pain?"

Grace leaned back against the settee. "There is less pain than before, but I don't think I will be dancing anytime soon."

"Nonsense, you just need the right partner."

"What is that supposed to mean?"

"Shall we test it?" He put the book down on the table and stood in front of her.

She blinked. "I—"

He held his hand out. "May I have this dance?"

Her heart stopped, then all at once it fluttered with anticipation at his request. She looked from his outstretched hand to his intense eyes. Grace's breath caught in her throat, and she tried to interpret her own feelings. "I should be delighted."

Her ungloved hand shook as she placed it in his, the tingling sensation spreading from her hand up through her shoulders as he helped her stand. He pulled her in close, holding her in his arms.

"You may lean on me," he said softly. "You should not

try to bear the entirety of your weight on your ankle."

"I should not wish to be a burden."

He brushed a small curl at the side of her face, tucking it behind her ear, and her eyes fluttered at their own accord at his touch. "Nonsense, Grace. The right partner will not think you a burden."

She knew she could trust Ollie. He had done everything to help her since she'd arrived. She leaned on him, keeping the weight off her ankle, and he adjusted his own stance to compensate.

His strong arms enveloped her. He smiled and began humming a tune as he slowly turned her around the room, helping her through the dance steps. The dance moved in half time, slower than she'd ever danced with a partner before.

She felt light and safe in Ollie's arms as they danced around the small room. He looked into her eyes with an emotion she couldn't name, and she realized just how much closer they were to each other.

She relaxed with his arms around her, and she put weight on her ankle testing it. She stumbled a little, but Ollie's arms were around her in an instant, as if he had anticipated her stumble. She held onto the lapels of his jacket. He smiled at her. "See, the right partner will help you."

Her breath caught. He held her, looking at her with adoration. She'd never felt so feminine or seen as she did in that moment. The way he looked at her made her believe that she truly was the belle of the ball—that she was beautiful and wanted. It was almost too much.

He stopped them in front of the fire. Still supporting her weight, he took one of her hands in his and brought it to his lips. He kissed the back of her hand, the sensation almost causing her to swoon. "See, your ankle will hold up for dancing with the right partner."

Her breathing came in short bursts. "Thank you for the dance," she said.

"It was my pleasure," he said, squeezing the hand he'd just kissed.

Grace's mouth went dry, and a swirl of emotions surrounded her. Was the duke such a partner? Attentive and caring? Ollie had been every bit the gentleman from the moment she'd arrived. Being in Ollie's arms had stirred an emotion inside of her, and then brought up another one on its heels. She didn't want to leave, because she didn't want to leave Ollie. A sadness pushed on her more than the pain in her ankle. After dancing with Ollie, would she want to dance with anyone else?

"Allow me," he said, helping her walk to the bedroom.

"I am content to take the settee tonight," she said.

He nodded. "You may at least have privacy to change."

After changing, Grace took out the pins and comb from her hair, letting her curls fall down her back. She braided her hair quickly, knowing that even though it was late, and she had an early morning tomorrow, she would be up for hours replaying every moment of their dance together.

CHAPTER TWELVE

The disconcerting quiet bothered Oliver as he brought the breakfast plates from the table to the kitchen. No storm, no wind, no howling. The dull morning light that filtered into the room from the window should have been a cheery sight, but the absence of the storm brought with it a foreboding feeling. "I do not think we can take your crutch with us," he said, after they'd eaten breakfast. "It will be cumbersome to ride with it."

Grace nodded. "Not to mention I wouldn't be able to explain where I received such a gift."

"That is very true."

"It was very kind of you to make it. I am indeed very grateful for the gift, even if I cannot take it with me," she said.

"Once you are better it wouldn't be very useful anyway.

We should try your boot on to see if you can wear it during the ride."

Grace nodded her ascent, and he worked at getting the boot on her foot. Grace gripped the sides of the wooden chair, but Oliver could tell that she was trying not to wince at the pain. She flinched again, and he pulled the boot away from her foot. "Your ankle will do better without the boot." He would pack it securely in her saddlebag.

"I can't simply ride a horse with only one boot," she said. "Perhaps I will just have to stay here with Apollo until I am fully healed." She patted the dog's head. Apollo closed his eyes happily in response, his tongue rolling out of his mouth.

Oliver shook his head. "As much as Apollo would love the attention, we must get you to your family and into the care of a physician who can make sure that everything is healing properly. I will carry you to your horse and help you mount. After that, we can wrap your foot in a blanket. It's the best we can do." He gave her the boot, and then picked her up.

Grace nodded. "You are right, of course."

Oliver took care to set everything to right in his hunting lodge. The fires were completely out; the food was stored.

Once they were out on the path, she said, "I shall miss this place. You have a very nice cottage, Ollie."

He looked back over his shoulder, following her line of sight. Covered with snow, and nestled with trees in the background, it was a very picturesque place—there was a peace and stillness about it. It was one of the reasons he liked being here. "Thank you, Grace."

In the stable, he helped Grace onto her mare, Honey, then carefully wrapped her ankle with a blanket.

He rubbed Poseidon's neck, speaking softly to the animal. He led both horses out of the stable, then secured the stable as well as the hunting lodge. Then he called to Apollo, who was sniffing at a nearby tree, and mounted his own horse.

"Apollo is coming with us?" Grace asked.

Oliver smiled. "Of course. He doesn't want to miss out on all the fun. It's an adventure this time of year, through the trees."

Grace nodded. "Will we take the road?"

Oliver shook his head. "Our most direct route will be through the forest. Going by the road would add more miles than we have daylight." Not to mention he didn't want to be seen riding through the countryside roads with Grace without a chaperone. It would raise too many questions, too many suspicions.

They rode through the countryside at a sedate pace. The entire earth was covered in snow, and Oliver didn't want any injuries on the horses due to unseen obstacles.

They fell into easy conversation—first about the weather, then about their childhood memories, and then about the upcoming Christmas season.

"Are you looking forward to the house party?" he asked Grace.

Grace was quiet for a moment. "I have been looking forward to it for weeks," she said, though her voice didn't sound as convincing. "Though I will miss ... that is to say, it is the first time I have been without my sisters. My youngest sister, Harmony, felt my leaving keenly. I have promised to write to her and all of them, and I hope it will be enough."

"But you've traveled before at Christmas time?" he asked, remembering some of the stories she told him.

"We have traveled, but only as a family. This is very different."

"You shall be with your cousin soon," he said. "That will be some consolation."

Grace nodded, but silence seemed to fill the space between them on the road.

Perhaps they were both lost in their own thoughts.

"What are your plans for the holidays?" she finally asked him. "Do you have ... that is to say, do you visit with anyone during the holidays?"

He took in a deep breath of the cold air. "Every year over the last decade has looked different," he said, not wanting to talk about the specifics of his memories unless they were stories from his youth. "This year I had planned to let the season come and go without too much fanfare." He waved his hand in the air. At least that had been his plan before Grace had stumbled into his life. Now—well now he wasn't sure how he saw the future. He was still figuring that part out.

"That seems a little lonely," she said. "Do you miss your family?"

A knot formed in his stomach, clenching tightly. "I do miss them. My father passed away several years ago. I hope in the next few years I will see my Mother and sisters again. My older sister married an Italian, and my mother went with her and my younger sisters to be there before the war. It was safer for them to stay there, instead of attempting to come back, and now it has become home for them. Although the current unrest has died down for the present, there is no telling if more won't come."

"That sounds lonely to be secluded," she said quietly.

It was lonely, especially when he considered all he'd lost. But the last few days had been some of the most enjoyable that he'd had in a long time. He wanted to voice his thoughts, but something held him back.

Apollo raced ahead of the horses, leaping through the snow, came bounding toward them, and then repeated the process.

"Apollo seems more excited than usual, if that were possible," Grace said, laughing.

The comment eased the tension from their heavy conversation about his family. "He loves this part of the country. It is one of his favorites."

"Is that so?"

"Yes. In the summertime, this area has quite a few squirrels. He never quite catches them, but he picks up their scent and chases them all through this area. We are nearly to your cousin's house," he said. "Once we crest this hill, you'll be able to see the outskirts of their estate."

She pulled on Honey's reins. "Thank you again for all of your help. And for everything."

"I was just doing what anyone would have," he said modestly.

"I very much doubt that. I shudder to think what would have happened if you didn't find me."

He looked at her pinched features, concerned with the worries of what might have been. "Then do not think on it. You are safe, and you will continue to heal once you are at your cousin's house." The path continued to be wide enough that he rode side by side next to her for most of the way.

"Ollie?" The way Grace said his name nearly undid him. He couldn't dwell on it.

He kept the reins loose in his hands. "Yes, Grace?"

"Shall we meet again?"

He held a breath. This was a moment of truth. Would he meet her again? He wanted to ... but ... he glanced at her, taking in her entire form, and the look in her eyes. "Does it matter if we meet again?"

Her eyebrows raised. "Of course it matters. You have become a dear friend. Surely, you must come into town every once in a while for supplies."

"I'm seldom in town," he said.

"Do you ever ... come to the balls?"

His heart sped up. Did she care if he, Ollie, came to balls? She was to pursue the duke—that had been her plan all along, and he needed to remember that. "It is far for me to travel."

"That is true. I know how dangerous the path can be, and to travel it after a ball ... it makes sense that you do not come." Her shoulders sagged slightly. "Perhaps you could come and stay for the house party. I am sure my cousin would be able to accommodate another guest."

He turned his horse to face her. "You do not want me to come."

"Of course I do."

He shook his head. He had to push through to the reality of their situation. "You cannot be serious. How would you explain that to your cousin?"

"I will come up with something. I am very clever."

"You are very clever, Grace," he admitted, his tone light. "But if anyone found out about the last several days, you'd be forced to marry me, remember?"

"That wouldn't be the worst thing," she said quietly. Then she laughed. "Yes, well we can't have that, can we?" She looked at him with such longing that for a moment he wondered if she really wouldn't mind marrying a man who lived in the woods.

He cleared his throat. "If we ever meet again, we would need to act like perfect strangers, waiting for an introduction. I couldn't insert myself into a house party without raising all kinds of questions."

"I wouldn't expect you to read me poetry every night." Her eyes widened. "You know what I mean."

"Grace, should you ever see me again, we must have a formal introduction before we can converse. You would not be able to ask your cousin if I could be invited to a house party."

"Perhaps I could just suggest ..."

He stopped her words. "You wouldn't be able to admit that you know me to anyone. Do you not see that it would cause a scandal?"

"Of course I am aware of that. If our situation was known, you'd be forced to marry me, and that would make you miserable."

He pulled his horse to a stop. He let her words sink in, but they rang untrue. "You would not make me miserable," he said.

She blinked, her jaw slacked. "That's good to know, I suppose."

"But you wouldn't want to be forced to marry me." He held his breath, knowing that her reaction to his statement was crucial in understanding where they stood.

CHAPTER THIRTEEN

Grace swallowed. She'd thought more than once about what it would be like to be married to Ollie over the past few days. The cottage was quaint. His attentions were doting, and full of tenderness. And she'd be a fool if she dwelt on any of it while she had a goal in front of her. It didn't matter what she thought of their time together. She had a responsibility to her family. To her sisters. She swallowed hard. "No one wants to be forced."

"Then we are in agreement," Ollie said, his face devoid of emotion.

"I was still hoping to introduce you to my relations," she said, as they neared the entrance of the drive.

Under the cover of trees, he turned his horse around, pulling Poseidon to a stop when they faced each other. "You know as well as I do that it wouldn't work."

She nodded. "I know." An uncomfortable lump formed

in her throat, and she forced her emotions to stay under control—at least as long as he was still near her.

His horse stamped the ground. "Grace, may I ask you a question?"

"Of course. You may always ask me any question. After all we are good friends. I hope that will not change even if we must pretend otherwise." Her heart squeezed as she said the words. Things would change. The end of this small, secluded path would mark the end of their time together.

"When you catch the duke, even if you do not love him —what then?"

"*When* I catch the duke? You are all confidence in me— don't you mean *if* I catch him?"

"My sweet Grace, after being in your company these last days, he would be a fool to let you go. He will recognize the jewel that you are and be completely smitten by you."

"That is very kind of you to say," she said, her heart breaking as he admitted the words.

"And if you don't love him?"

She sighed, her gaze unfocused ahead of her as poetry readings and laughter filtered through her conscious. "I hope it will not be a loveless match for long, after all now that I know ..." She stopped herself before she said something she wouldn't be able to take back, that time with *him* had changed her outlook, and she didn't want to settle. "What I mean to say is a wise friend recently told me that love was worth the heartache. And I believe I can trust him on that." She looked into his blue eyes, which appeared darker under the cover of the trees. "I do hope we meet again," she said.

"I hope that too," he said slowly, as if measuring his words.

She took hold of the fact that he was thinking about it. He didn't immediately dismiss the idea. All at once her words rushed together. "And will you consider coming to the public Christmas ball at the assembly? It is in town and open to the public. The house party will be attending it too. Will you come?"

"I shouldn't want to intrude on your plans with other guests."

She waved her hand in the air, the idea buzzing around her like a nuisance. "Oh you won't. Besides, I should like a proper dance with you, if you will have me." Her cheeks warmed as she thought of the way he'd held her in his arms last night, twirling her around like she was floating on air. What would it be like to have her feet on the ground dancing with him, sans her injured ankle? She wanted to find out, not just imagine that.

"I should like nothing more than to dance with you at a ball."

She smiled, hearing the truth in his words, knowing that in that moment she looked forward to dancing with him more than the duke or anyone else who would be there. "Then I shall hold you to it." Her breath caught at her own forwardness. What was she thinking? She was walking a dangerous line between her duty and her feelings. "After all, friends can dance with one another, can they not? Of course they can."

"And we are friends," he said. His horse side-stepped. "Grace, if circumstances had been different, would you have considered ... would we have suited?"

The cavity around her heart tremored at the question. "We do suit, Ollie. But—"

"I am not wealthy enough." He looked to the sky.

Her heart squeezed inside of her. The very idea of drawing breath felt difficult. "That is not it at all, Ollie." They had been dancing around the attraction and connection. But it had never been acknowledged directly. It was easier to think of it in terms of poetry that was beautiful to listen to and not to analyze or apply. "It is not *your* circumstance, but *mine*." Tears threatened at the corners of her eyes, but she willed them to stay in place. "If *I* was in a different position, things would be different."

Hope seemed to glitter in his eyes. "You would consider me as a suitor?"

"If I had the ability to choose, I would want nothing more." She looked at the path before him. Saying the words aloud made it sound as if she only cared about money. But that was not the case at all. "But I have my family to think of. I have a responsibility to help them, and I have committed to that course. I cannot let them down. I must give my sisters the ability to have the opportunity I cannot take for myself."

"You are an incredible woman to put your family first in such a way," he said sincerely.

She took off the borrowed riding gloves she'd used. She couldn't keep them. She held them out to Ollie. He reached out and accepted his gloves from her, then tucked them under one arm. Then he took her hand in his own. Turning her hand over, he traced his fingers over where the cuts had been on her palm. Gently, he lifted her hand to his lips and kissed her palm.

Grace closed her eyes, letting the sensation of his lips on her skin fill her, even as her heart tried to remain intact. Tears pooled in her eyes, threatening to spill. Her throat tightened, refusing to let words out without emotion. "I was naive to think that because it was a sacrifice that I'm willing to make that it would not affect me. I didn't know what I was saying before. I didn't realize how much of a sacrifice this would be."

He squeezed her hand, his face a mirror of her own emotions. "Grace, I need to tell you something."

"What is it?"

In the distance, the muffled sound of horses pulling a carriage could be heard. Apollo barked at the interruption, and the moment between them dissipated.

Ollie shifted atop his horse, looking around warily. "I will take my leave of you, Grace. We must part before we are spotted."

"Yes, we must." There was a small piece of Grace that wanted to be spotted. It would surely ruin her reputation and create a scandal beyond measure, but being forced to marry Ollie—would that almost solve her problems? Almost.

"If you follow this road all the way to the back of the house, you'll find the stables, and likely a groomsman or stable hand that can assist you."

"Are you heading back to the cottage tonight?" It was getting dark. Would he make it safely?

He looked at the horizon and then back to her. "I am heading home."

"Be safe. The woods can be dangerous," she said, trying to lighten the mood that seemed to grow heavy between them.

He nodded. "That is wise advice."

"I look forward to our dance, if you will come to the Christmas ball," she said.

His eyes brightened. "I should like that. Goodbye, Grace."

"Goodbye, Ollie. Thank you for ... everything." A lump formed in her throat.

Poseidon stomped at the ground, but Ollie moved his horse closer to Grace. He took Grace's hand in his again, this time bowing over it and placing a kiss on her knuckles. "It was my pleasure, Grace," he said, whispering the words. Then he clicked at his horse, and they left in the opposite direction.

Grace blinked rapidly and urged Honey forward. She glanced back at Ollie's retreating form. Her pulse raced as she admired him. He sat tall on his horse. He was clearly well trained at riding. Her breath hitched when he turned back around and their gazes locked. He smiled at her and held up his hand in farewell. She nodded, then turned around and headed up the drive.

Honey only made it a few steps before Grace's gaze was drawn backward again. Ollie did not turn around again, though Grace glanced back several more times hoping to catch his gaze. Then the pathway turned, and she lost sight of him completely.

Grace wanted to ride after Ollie, but she knew it would not be proper. She reminded herself that nothing about her friendship with Ollie had followed the societal norms for interaction. But Ollie had always been a perfect gentleman to her. She released the breath she'd been holding once Ollie was no longer in sight.

Was there a way her parents could understand? She knew she couldn't tell anyone about the first time they met, or about how he'd rescued her. They'd be forced to marry after such news spread. But was that perhaps a way to solve the problem of her conflicted heart? No. Adding scandal to a marriage wouldn't be the way forward. And her marriage then wouldn't help her family, only hinder them.

She sighed. He knew her situation. She'd told him in great detail about her family, about each of her sisters, and about their financial situation. She shook her head at the folly of revealing so much about herself. Perhaps it was her fall that had loosened her tongue so much. Perhaps if she'd revealed less, the hurt she'd seen in his eyes wouldn't have been there.

She made her way to the stables, and as Ollie predicted there was someone there to help her. It was a flurry of frenzied mayhem after that.

Susan came out to greet her, practically running toward her before she'd gotten off her horse. "Oh, my dear sweet cousin! You're here on horseback?" She began giving orders to servants. "Where are your trunks?"

"Have they not arrived yet?" Grace asked.

"No. We have had no one along here in days. Of course, we have had a bad storm. How are you here without your trunks?"

She breathed a sigh of relief that her trunks hadn't arrived. She and Ollie's reputations were both still intact. If her trunks hadn't come, then her cousin had had no need to worry about her. "I went on ahead of the carriage," she said.

Susan nodded, but then went back to telling servants what to do. "What happened to your foot?"

"Just a slightly twisted ankle, but I am quite alright, as you see." Grace smiled.

Susan called for a stable hand, and once they were in the stable, he helped Grace from her horse.

"Some guests have already arrived. Although the house party hasn't officially started, we are having a merry time." Susan offered her arm, and Grace leaned more heavily than she would have liked to on her cousin. "Are you truly alright, Grace?"

Grace tried to stand up straighter and not limp as much. "There is no cause for alarm. I am getting better."

Susan eyed her, then called for a servant to fetch a walking stick. It was brought and Grace was able to support her own weight with the tool.

"That is very kind of you," Grace said, though she missed the feel of the smooth, hand carved wood of her crutch. "I'm sure I shall be alright now."

"All guest rooms have been readied. I will show you to yours and then you can take a bath and clean up." Susan led Grace up the stairs. Each step felt arduous and foreign to her, but she made it through the difficulty. After all, there were no steps in Ollie's cottage.

"This room looks beautiful," Grace said when they entered her chamber.

"It is one of our finest guest bedrooms," Susan said. "As your trunks have not arrived yet, I will send a servant with a few changes of clothes from my own wardrobe while you are waiting for yours. I will see that they draw you a bath."

"Thank you, Susan. You are most kind to me."

"I will send for the doctor," Susan said. She embraced her cousin. "I'm so happy you have arrived safely."

"I am as well. I should very much like to hear your plans for the house party in full."

Susan nodded. "Once you are bathed and in bed resting that ankle I will send for a tray and we can talk then."

Molly, an upper servant, came to attend Grace. After having a bath, Grace was immediately whisked into a nightgown and put into her bed. Soon after a knock sounded on her door. Grace pushed aside the thoughts of how familiar this felt, being in a bed, while Ollie had knocked on the door at night. She glanced to the side of the room where a shelf full of an exhaustive amount of reading on the natural world should have been, but in its place was a large hearth blazing.

"Come in," Grace said, pushing away thoughts of Shakespeare and a deep voice reading her sonnets.

Susan smiled as she entered. "I have sent for the doctor. He will be here soon to check on your ankle."

"I believe it will be fine. There is no need to make such a fuss," Grace said.

"Of course there is. You are my honored guest, and our house party is upon us. You will want to be feeling your very best, if you mean to catch anyone's eye."

Grace looked at her cousin curiously. "I take it you have heard from my parents."

Susan nodded. "I know you have secured a proposal, but that you are still undecided on it."

Grace filled in the information her parents had left out.

"I have half a dozen gentlemen coming and the same number of ladies. You shall have your pick of any of them. I will make all the arrangements, and as you have not brought a maid along, I will provide one for you. The schedule will be rigorous, with activities planned for the entire week."

Grace knew that this would be the case, but in hearing plans for the schedule, she suddenly grew tired, wanting the comforts of a slower pace—perhaps in a cottage.

"Who are the guests?" Grace asked.

Susan rattled off the names and stations of all the guests coming. It would seem that nothing was left undone.

"And what of your neighbor?" Grace asked. "Will the duke be in attendance?"

Susan shook her head. "I am sorry to say that since I wrote you last, the duke has declined my invitation. He is presently from home, although, I thought I saw him riding earlier across the land between our two properties."

Grace's heart sank. "So the duke will not be here?"

"No. It almost set the numbers to be uneven, but another has also been called away, due to the ailing health of a relative, so Lady Josephine will not be joining us either."

"That is a shame," Grace said. "I'm not sure what I should do." She looked around wondering where Ollie's blanket that had wrapped her foot had gone. "The clothes I was wearing when I came here ..."

Susan smiled. "I sent all of your clothes to be laundered. They will be returned to you tomorrow."

Grace nodded. "There was also a blanket with them."

Susan nodded. "I'm sure it will also be laundered. Where did you find a blanket to wrap your foot with anyway? Surely you didn't bring that in your saddlebag?"

Grace smiled. "A good Samaritan lent it to me."

"That was kind," Susan said. "And I'm so glad you were able to find our house so quickly."

Grace nodded. "I found a friendly face who made sure I was going in the right direction and that I made it through the snow safely."

"I see. Well the important thing is you are here now." Susan squeezed Grace's hand. "Now, tell me about this arrangement you have, and how we can best find you a match before the end of this house party."

Grace and Susan talked for the next quarter of an hour, until there was another knock at the door and the doctor entered. The gray-haired man made his way to Grace's bedside and after asking a few questions, looked at Grace's ankle.

After examining it, the doctor said, "Thankfully you do not have a break in the bone. But you do have a sprained ankle."

"How long will it take to heal?" Susan asked the question on Grace's mind.

"I'd guess the recovery will be quick if you let it rest for the next week or two." The doctor then gave a few remedies and made Grace a poultice.

When the doctor left the room, Susan turned to Grace. "A week or two is not so bad. We shall make sure you stay off your ankle as much as possible before the house party, and I'm sure that will do the trick."

"I hope you're right," Grace said.

"Watch and see, it will be the idea of dancing with the

duke at the Christmas ball that will heal you." Susan laughed. "He is bound to come to the assembly if he is in town."

Grace laughed at her cousin's remark, doubting that simply thinking about the duke at the Christmas ball would help her ankle heal. Her mind instantly turned to Ollie—would the prospect completely healing in time to dance with him again create some sort of instant healing. "Perhaps I will look forward to the Christmas ball then."

"The duke is an excellent dancer," Susan said. "I'm sure I've told you that before. I've partnered him a couple of times, and it has never been an unpleasant experience."

"I don't know much about him," Grace admitted. Except for what Ollie told her, but she wasn't going to reveal that to her cousin. "Perhaps you can tell me all about the guests who are coming."

"I will tell you what I know of each of them," she said, taking the seat beside Grace's bed. "There are plenty of eligible bachelors here, and you will have a grand time with all of them. They are all wealthy and titled. Not as wealthy as a duke, perhaps, and not as high of a rank, but perhaps you'll be able to snag one of them instead, and give up the idea of the duke."

Grace listened to her cousin talk about the different invited guests, but she hardly heard a word. The idea of snagging someone else, even the duke, had lost much of its appeal. She still didn't like the idea of marrying someone twice her age, but instead of thinking of the party guests she thought of blue eyes and a jaw covered in stubble. Snagging someone else did not appeal to her in the slightest, unless it was a particular someone who lived remotely. Grace shook her head, wishing to let go of the silly notion.

"Well if you do not like Mr. Ashworth, there is a son of an earl that would do well," her cousin said, thinking that Grace had shaken her head to her cousin, instead of herself.

Grace tried to pay attention, but as Susan spoke of each gentleman, her heart was not in it. Of course it wasn't. She had to marry for money, for status, for a title. She was the one who would help her sisters have a choice. She loved all of them, and this was her responsibility. Would a marquess or an earl do for her family? Would her parents approve of that and not require her to marry a man who was twice her age if they didn't agree to help them out financially?

She swallowed. If an earl without financial help was good enough for her family, could someone of even lower standing be acceptable too? She shook her head. It was impossible. She required the connection to be able to help her sisters. She would be allowing them a choice. They would be able to marry whoever they wanted to, be it a marquess or a farmer. And she would marry to secure their choices. She would do it happily and with grace. But that didn't stop Ollie's eyes from appearing in her mind each time she closed her eyes, or tried to picture someone her cousin was describing.

CHAPTER FOURTEEN

Oliver stayed hidden in the trees while Grace had made her way to the stables. He wanted to make sure that someone helped her before he completely abandoned her to her cousin. He knew that she would be able to heal and recover better at her cousin's house, so why was he feeling a loss?

He pulled on the reins and turned his horse around with a few clicks of his tongue. His horse stamped with excitement at the familiarity of the surrounding area. But he could not go home yet, though Oliver had been hours on the saddle, it had been at a slow pace. Both he and Poseidon needed a little more exercise.

They rode through a small clump of trees. Once they thinned and dispersed behind him, he gave Poseidon his head as they raced across the countryside making their way home to Cliffton Manor.

Instead of handing his horse over to the stable hands, he dismounted and led Poseidon into the stables, taking care of his horse's needs before finally exiting the stables. Having been without a stable hand at his hunting lodge, he wasn't ready to turn over the care of Poseidon just yet.

Remington, the butler, bowed to him. "Your Grace, it is good to have you home again."

He took in his surroundings. "It is always good to be home."

"Had we known you would be cutting your time at the hunting lodge short, the servants would have all turned out for you."

Oliver put a hand on the man's shoulders. Remington had known Oliver since he was a young boy. "It is quite alright, Remington. There is no need in this weather, and as you say, I've returned home early." Oliver momentarily glanced back the way he'd come, searching for the outline of his neighbor's house in the distance. It had never bothered him before that he couldn't always see the roof and chimneys through the trees.

"Dinner shall be served whenever you wish it." Remington took Oliver's hat and coat.

Oliver nodded. "As soon as it is convenient, I should like to see my steward."

Mrs. Dodds burst into the entryway, giving a hasty curtsy to Oliver, and then fussing over him like a mother hen. Though Oliver was the master of the house, Mrs. Dodds ran the details of the house with precision. After asking him about his trip, she said, "You look cold. I will prepare a tray for you to be served after your bath." Then she curtsied, as if the idea to bathe and change had been his idea instead of hers. Oliver smiled. Mrs. Dodds was a force to be reckoned with.

AN HOUR LATER, OLIVER MET WITH HIS STEWARD, MR. Cordon, in his office. After being briefed on matters that required Oliver's attention, he changed the subject. "What were the details of the Christmas house party?" He drummed his fingers along his desk as if he was disinterested in the answer.

Mr. Cordon straightened in his chair, clearly not buying the act of nonchalance. "I thought you were away at the hunting lodge because you didn't want to be home during the Christmas house parties. Wasn't that your specific request?"

Oliver ran his hand through his slightly damp hair. Would Grace like this version of him? He rubbed at his clean-shaven jaw, still itchy. "I've changed my mind. I want to be there. Is it too late to accept the house party invitation?"

His steward looked shocked, as if Oliver had requested something unsavory. Then he cleared his throat. "Your Grace, you are a duke. You may do anything that you want."

He looked like he would say more, but remained reserved. The effort looked like it pained him.

Oliver stood from his chair and paced the room. "I should like to attend," he said.

The steward nodded. "Very well. I am sure I can make the necessary arrangements."

Oliver stopped his pacing when he noticed Mr. Cordon's confused look. "What is it?"

His steward shifted uncomfortably. "It is nothing, Your Grace. I only wondered if there was a particular ... that is to say, you are back earlier than planned. It is not like you to seek out social gatherings at this time of year." He paused, then pushed on. "Is there a particular event that you want to participate in?"

Oliver waved his hand in the air. Events didn't matter so much as the particular person that he wished to see, but he knew he couldn't admit that without alluding to what could be deemed a scandal. "No particular event," Oliver said.

Mr. Cordon nodded, his face a mask devoid of emotion, expertly hiding his true thoughts.

"Do you think it's a bad idea that I go to the house party?" Oliver asked his steward. Though in his employ, he valued Mr. Cordon's opinions, which was why he brought the matter to him in the first place.

"No, of course not. As I said, you may attend any function in society almost by rule, whether or not you have an invitation. I only wondered because it was so out of character for you."

Oliver nodded in agreement. It was out of character. Completely out of character. How would Grace take the shock of it? Would she like the fact that he had, in a way, taken her up on the offer to join the house party? He paced again. Something felt off. As the duke, he would not have been afforded the same familiarity with Grace at the house party that the hunting lodge had provided.

There was a very strong chance that it wouldn't turn out well for him if he attended the house party invitation after declining it. Perhaps what he needed was to ease Grace into the idea of his true identity. He'd almost told her in the woods, right before he'd dropped her off. But somehow the moment of her falling for him while she only knew him as a man living in a rustic cottage had given him pause.

In that brief moment under the shelter of the snowy trees, she'd seemed to care more about dancing with Ollie than about meeting the duke. It was still a perplexing situation to be in.

"On second thought, perhaps I shouldn't go to the house party, after all."

"Of course, Your Grace. If pressed, I will explain your presence back at Cliffton Manor due to the business being resolved earlier than planned."

Oliver waved a hand in the air. Being in the woods had seemed urgent when avoiding social functions. And without that choice he never would have met Grace the way he did. And that would have been a shame. "I believe I will ride out again to the hunting lodge tomorrow," he said, forming the idea in his mind. He wanted to give the poetry book to Grace. "I won't be gone long, but I need to pick up something I left there."

"Very well," Mr. Cordon said. "I shall make the necessary arrangements."

"I will attend the Christmas Ball at the assembly room this year."

"Shall I send for something from your London house? Or order you a new waistcoat perhaps?"

"There is no need. I have enough to choose from here."

"Very good, Your Grace."

CHAPTER FIFTEEN

Sunlight glinted off the blanket of snow covering the back fields. Each member of the house party was outside, dressed warmly, and getting ready to ride. When Grace had suggested the evening before that she might take her horse outside for some exercise after so many days in the stables, she hadn't anticipated that the idea would catch hold of everyone in attendance.

Indeed she had said it as an excuse to get out of the afternoon's activity and find some much needed solitude. Large gatherings did not bother her, but she found she missed the time quietly tucked away in the corner of a forest. Susan had taken the idea and proposed it to everyone, and now here they all were on the grounds, wrapped in brilliant jeweled-toned cloaks.

One by one the gentlemen mounted their horses as they

were brought to them. The women required help, but the process only took a few moments.

Susan pulled her mare in line with Grace. "I hope you don't mind the company out here."

"Not at all," Grace said, pushing down some of her disappointment that her solitary time was encroached upon. She would have time enough to be alone after the house party came to an end. "Your house party is quite the success," Grace said.

Susan beamed at the praise. "It has been most enjoyable to plan."

"Thank you for having me. I am sure life at home would have been quite dull by comparison." There were endless activities every day—games, musicales, cards, and dancing.

"Have you developed an attachment to anyone particular since arriving?" Susan asked, wiggling her eyebrows up and down.

Ollie's bright blue eyes came immediately to mind, and heat flooded her cheeks. "I can't think who you would mean," she said. As Susan had predicted the duke had not come to the house party, and though Grace was polite to all of the guests, her heart wasn't up for the challenge of finding other prospects among the party.

"I have noticed that Lord Stanton has been paying you particular attention. Might there be a chance for something there?"

Grace gave her cousin a small smile. Susan knew Grace's plight and her circumstance, but she had yet to learn about Ollie, or how Grace couldn't get her mind off the man who had rescued her in the woods, and then cared for her during the storm.

Perhaps it was only the realization that she could have died out there in the woods, that she'd been foolish to seek her independence from her chaperone to enjoy riding on her mare, but it was more than that. He'd rescued her from the storm, but he'd also unknowingly rescued her heart as well.

If her heart still was with him, how could she choose another now, so soon?

Grace couldn't explain any of those thoughts to Susan, but she finally said, "Lord Stanton is a very kind gentleman. He is attentive and a good conversationalist."

"Those are all excellent things in his favor," Susan said as they rode. "And he is handsome. The two of you make an excellent picture together."

"I enjoy Lord Stanton's company," Grace said smoothly.

"Might he be someone you consider?" Susan asked again, with more than a little interest behind the question.

"Perhaps," Grace said, with less assurance than her prior statements.

The party moved down the hill, toward the trees. In the distance, Grace watched a horse gallop across the countryside. The rider and horse looked so much like Ollie and Poseidon that Grace gasped, startling Honey. She reined her in, calming the beast below her. She stroked Honey's neck speaking softly.

Susan eyed Grace's horse skeptically. "Your horse is

quite jittery, between throwing you before and her movements just now ..."

"She is fine. It wasn't her fault she was startled when I was thrown. And it was my fault now. I thought I saw someone in the distance who ..." She stopped before she said Ollie's name or that he'd rescued her. "Who I once knew, that is all."

Susan turned in the direction Grace was looking and squinted against the sunlight. "It is hard to see much with the sun shining so brightly on this snow. For a moment, I thought I saw the duke riding his horse, but that is impossible, as he is out of town until Christmas."

Grace looked back to where the small horse and rider had disappeared from view, somewhere in the line of trees. Perhaps everyone only saw what they wanted to see—a reflection of their own imagination. Grace had thought of Ollie, while Susan had thought of the duke. In reality, all gentlemen looked rather similar to each other when they were on horseback galloping across a field. Too similar to make any kind of pronouncement on who it was when they were so far away, backlit, and hidden by the tree line.

She dismissed the thought. She was not going to think of Ollie again. Not going to imagine him again. It did no good to think on their time together. She had no way to contact him. No way to find him again. And even if she had his direction—what would that signify? She could not call on him the way she could a friend or neighbor.

She had invited him to come to the ball, but the

Christmas ball was still over a week away. She wished it were tomorrow, and that he would actually come. She would know in a week.

"Lord Stanton," Susan called from atop her horse. "Would you mind keeping Grace company while I ride ahead to check on the rest of our party?"

Lord Stanton tipped his hat, riding toward the two women.

"You may thank me later," Susan whispered to Grace. "He is quite the catch."

Grace breathed in the cold air and did her best to smile at Lord Stanton as he approached. She forced herself to not compare everything he did or said to Ollie, but it took a considerable effort.

CHAPTER SIXTEEN

G race smoothed down her jade green ball gown. Susan had insisted that Grace borrow the gown after she'd inspected all of Grace's trunks. The cut of the borrowed dress was flattering on her. She walked into the assembly room on Lord Stanton's arm. His waistcoat was the exact same shade of green as her dress. She had to admit, as Susan had before, that they created a nice picture together. He led her toward the dance floor and they took their places to join the quadrille.

Grace scanned the room for a pair of blue eyes, but Ollie was not among the crowd. Lord Stanton kept the conversation going between them, talking of his lands, and the horses he had a mind to buy when he was next in Town. Grace listened, but he rarely sought or needed a response. She smiled politely at her partner, wondering if dancing was a sign of how married life would be, if she would enjoy playing the part of a doting wife, simply to secure her family's comfort. Two weeks ago, she'd wanted nothing else. But then those blue eyes haunted her, making her rethink her own happiness. Was it possible that she could be afforded happiness in marriage too? She swallowed down the thoughts and focused on Lord Stanton for the rest of the dance.

After three more sets with other gentlemen from the house party, Grace asked for a glass of lemonade. Mr. Carrington obliged her, bringing her a drink.

"I know you have promised this next set to Miss Harcourt," Grace said to Mr. Carrington. "I am going to sit out this dance."

Mr. Carrington nodded. "Is there anything else I can do for you?"

Grace shook her head. "I shall be quite comfortable here. Thank you, Mr. Carrington."

Mr. Carrington bowed, then escorted Miss Harcourt to the dance floor.

Grace sipped her lemonade and scanned the room. She didn't recognize all of the faces, but she didn't see the set of blue eyes she was searching for. She sighed. She hadn't allowed herself to truly believe that he would come so far just to dance with her, but she felt the hope swirl with disappointment and spread through her anyway. The corners of her eyes pricked, threatening to burn with disappointment. She blinked rapidly. She would not cry. She would not. The withdrawing rooms were set up on the exact opposite side of the room from where she was. She needed an escape.

Spying the doors to the terrace, she made her way quickly, letting herself outside. The chilly air hit her with force, stealing her breath, but also calming down the wave of emotions. She gulped in the air, allowing it to cool her nerves. The stinging sensation next to her eyes slowly receded.

She rubbed her gloved arms, feeling the cold through them. She looked at the other couples on the terrace, each in wraps or shawls. She'd left hers inside. She wouldn't stay out very long. She just needed a moment to herself. The snow-covered scenery before her felt like home. The moon glinted off the snow, making the grounds feel brighter than they otherwise would be at night. Torch lights were set up through the small garden behind the assembly room. It didn't sprawl out like an estate, and Grace couldn't see anyone below her on the paths.

Grace looked up at the stars and sighed. She'd never seen the stars in the forest. The weather had not made that possible. Laughter died away behind her and she heard sounds from the ballroom growing louder. Out of the corner of her eye she could tell that the other couples were rejoining the party inside.

Grace took a few more steadying breaths and looked up at the sky one last time. The outdoors had reminded her of her time with Ollie. Everything reminded her of her time with Ollie. Their time together had been as fleeting as a dream. And that time was over. Even if he had shown up to the ball, dancing with Ollie here wouldn't change the fact that nothing could come of it.

If she didn't find a match and have a proposal in hand before she left her cousin's house, she'd committed to marrying the earl, and she wouldn't go back on her word. She loved her family too much to let them live in the fallen state of financial ruin they found themselves in. She would sacrifice, just like she said she would. But until she met Ollie she hadn't truly understood what that meant—this sacrifice was greater than she had originally anticipated.

"I shall do it," she whispered to herself and into the night. "I shall allow all of them the happiness I cannot claim for myself." She shivered, and the night air soaked into her more. It was time to head back into the ballroom. Time to face her reality, and time to figure out what she should do next in her life.

She turned, and came face to face with the first man she'd hoped to see and the very last she'd expected. "Ollie?"

He gave her a slight bow, his smile widening at her. He was clean shaven, his hair a picture of perfection with curls waving over his forehead. She didn't realize he could become more handsome than she remembered or imagined.

Emotion overcame her at seeing her friend again, she stepped quickly toward him. Longing filled her with such force, and she wanted to throw her arms around his neck and embrace him. Instead she kept her arms at her side, though no one else was out on the terrace anymore. "Ollie, you came! I'm so glad you did. I have missed you." Heat rose to her neck and cheeks at her forward admission, scaring away the coldness she'd felt only moments ago.

He lifted an eyebrow. His eyes held her gaze with intensity. "Have you?"

She nodded.

"How is your ankle?"

"It is much better. And it continues to feel better every day."

"I am glad to hear it. Did you come in a large group this evening?"

Grace nodded. "The majority of the house party came tonight."

"How have you been enjoying the activities?" he asked.

Grace smiled at the easy way he asked questions. It reminded her of nights by the fire as they talked together. But she knew what he was really asking. He wanted to know about who she was spending her time with. She could feel it instinctively, the way he watched her so carefully. "My cousin has planned everything down to the finest details. I have enjoyed my time. It is different than I anticipated however."

"How so?"

"Not everyone who was invited is in attendance." She shivered again, then lowered her voice. "The duke did not accept the invitation. I suppose that was to be expected."

Ollie opened his mouth as if to say something then

looked back to the terrace doors. "Grace, I have something I would like to talk to you about."

Grace rubbed her arms where her gloves did not cover. "Yes, Ollie?"

He glanced around them once more, then said, "You look cold."

"I see your tact is the same as ever, telling a woman what she precisely does not want to hear."

"Or perhaps you can see that I am aware of your needs, and I won't beat around the bush to tell you I can see them."

"Touché, Ollie. I suppose it would be best to return to the ball."

Ollie looked hesitant, but then nodded. "I wonder, Grace, if you will do me the honor of the next set?"

Grace's heart thudded in her chest. Her mouth went dry as she tried to speak to the person she'd been thinking about since the last time she'd seen him. "You ... *want* to dance with me?"

His intense blue eyes looked into hers as if they were trying to memorize everything they were seeing. "Of course I want to dance with you, Grace. You are the only reason I am here tonight."

Excitement bubbled around Grace, and she allowed herself to be swallowed up in the moment, even if it was only her reality for a short time. "I would love nothing more."

Ollie took her hand and looped it through his arm, his eyes trained on her as if she would vanish if he didn't keep looking at her. He put his hand atop hers as she rested her hand on his forearm, feeling his muscle and strength through his jacket. Unlike when she was being escorted by Lord Stanton, a hundred emotions pulled at Grace as she walked the final length of the terrace with Ollie. She was hot and cold at the same time. Nerves bounced around between excitement and anticipation.

She leaned into him, brushing her shoulder against him, and drinking in the smell of cedar and mint—the scent that was uniquely Ollie. She allowed him to lead her inside and to the dance floor, savoring the closeness between them.

"I need to speak to you first," Ollie said, squeezing her hand beneath his, pulling her away from where he'd been leading her.

"The next set is beginning right now," Grace said, pulling Ollie the rest of the way toward the dance floor. So excited as she was to see her friend here, she didn't want to miss a single second of dancing with him. "Surely, whatever you wish to say can be said on the dance floor."

She smiled at her friend, and tried to squash her earlier thoughts. Seeing Ollie again meant that she knew she couldn't agree to an arranged marriage. She wanted a connection like the one she felt with the man across from her. She didn't need a duke or an earl. She wanted something deeper than status or comfort.

CHAPTER SEVENTEEN

Oliver Hayward, Duke of Norfolk, bowed to his partner, Grace, from across the line. He could feel the stares from everyone in the room. This was decidedly a very dangerous idea to come here like this. He had appeared fashionably late, and had stayed in the shadows for a set watching Grace dance with other partners.

When she'd sat out for a set, he'd hoped to make his way to her, but she'd gone outside before he was able to reach her. He'd tried to follow after her, and had been swarmed by several women all begging for dances for their daughters. It was then that Oliver had gone out through the front door, and come around through an adjoining path to the back of the terrace. Not wanting to draw more attention to himself, he'd waited until the other couples on the balcony had left before he approached Grace.

He'd wanted to talk outside with her for longer, but

she'd been cold, and the protective part of him that had saved her in the forest wanted to make sure that she was safe and inside again, not outside exposed to the elements.

As they twirled around for the first move of the dance, he supported her, only slightly lifting her off her toes, reminiscent of the way he'd done when they were dancing together in his hunting lodge.

Grace's eyes widened for a fraction of a second before she smiled at him.

"I agree with you," he said.

"On what subject, pray tell?" she asked.

"You once said you were an excellent dancer."

"Did I? How boastful of me to admit it," she said, their easy rapport coming quickly with each step.

"Yes, at the time I thought it was very boastful."

"There you go, saying things too bluntly for proper society." She smiled at him playfully.

His heart skipped a beat. "Shouldn't you like to hear statements bluntly, even if it lacks tact? After all, I should think you would prefer truth over just flattering words."

"So you do not mean to flatter me?"

He spun her around, pulling her closer than was absolutely necessary. He lowered his voice. "Make no mistake about it, my dear Grace. I mean to flatter you, but it is not for the sake of flattery alone that I tell you the truth of the matter."

She swallowed, and a slight blush formed on her cheeks.

"You always speak your mind, so I do not think that you flatter me insincerely."

"And you are an excellent dancer, I quite agree." He pulled her closer. "I had my suspicions when we first danced, but it was quite hard to tell with that ankle at the time."

Her cheeks colored. "I am glad you did not judge my skills earlier. After all, I could barely walk at the time."

"Perhaps it was all about having the right partner when you're dancing," he said, wondering if she would catch his full meaning.

She inhaled sharply. "Everyone is staring at us."

He shook his head. "I believe it is *you* everyone is looking at. You've captured the whole room without exception." Including himself.

"Do I have a chance at winning people over with my dancing skills, do you think?" She looked at him thoughtfully.

Did she mean him, or the duke? Or someone entirely different? Somehow the answer to the question was based more on which one she was thinking about in the moment. "I believe you will win over many," he said vaguely. "But excellent dancing requires an excellent partner."

They were apart for a few steps, but when they came back together and promenaded hand in hand, she whispered, "Are you staying in town?"

His chest tightened. "Why would you ask that?"

"Only that it is a very long way back to your house

tonight, and without a carriage it seems most uncomfortable."

"You're worried for my safety? I am quite able to take care of myself."

She smiled and shook her head playfully. "Not your safety. But you have a beautiful horse. I would hate for Poseidon to get lost and spooked."

He smiled at her, enjoying the banter between them like he had when they'd been together in his hunting lodge. He found himself wanting to rise to the challenge with her around. He liked her fire and her drive for life. And he sensed in their conversation a deeper concern that she had for him. She didn't want him, or his horse, to be in a situation like she'd been in.

"I have a confession to make," he whispered, hoping no one around them caught their conversation. "I shall not be going back to ... the cottage ... as you call it, for quite some time."

She raised her eyebrows, interest sparking in her eyes. "And why is that?"

"Only that I have reasons to be in town more now than I did before."

"In London?"

"No. Here."

"And what reasons do you have for such a move?" she asked.

He searched her face, contemplating how bold he should be. According to her, he'd come a long way, so she didn't know. She hadn't made the connection. Part of him wanted to keep it that way, but he knew it was impossible. "I think you already know the answer to that. I have something I must confess to you," he said, not wanting to wait until a secluded moment at the end of the dance. He needed to tell her now, help her understand how this connection between them aligned with what she wanted, and what he needed.

"Ollie, I am flattered by your attentions. But you know my family situation ..."

"You have your heart set on the duke." He set the stage perfectly for her to understand who he was, but she interrupted him before he could continue.

She wrinkled her brow. "Yes. No. I don't even know the man yet. But my family is depending on me. I cannot let them down, no matter how much—" She shook her head, not finishing the sentence.

The dance pulled them apart again, and when he was once again next to her, he said, "I understand familial duty. But, Grace—"

Pain filled Grace's eyes. "Perhaps we can finish this conversation after the dance," she said.

He nodded, aware of the many prying ears around him for the first time. They danced the rest of the set in silence, and though she smiled at him, there was something different in her eyes, a sadness that had not been there before. His own pulse raced at the sight. Soon enough he would be able to wipe the worried look from her eyes.

The dance ended, and he escorted her off the dance

floor. He held onto her delicate hand with a firm grip, never wishing to let it go. Bowing over her hand, he placed a small kiss on the back of her gloved knuckles.

Grace smiled, but didn't make eye contact, only focused on his cravat while she whispered, "Thank you for the dance, Ollie."

"It was my pleasure. There is something which I wish to discuss with you," he said.

She bit her lip. "I do not think there is more we need to discuss about the matter."

"If you would let me explain—" he said. And then, without warning the entire room seemed to descend upon the corner where they stood.

"Your Grace, it is good to see you in town," a woman said, coming up to them.

"Will you be here long?" another gentleman asked.

Oliver stood a little taller, bowing to the people in front of him. "Thank you, Mrs. Williams. It is good to be in town. I shall be here until the start of the Season, and then I will remove to London, Lord Hampton."

"That is good to hear, Your Grace," Lord Hampton said.

He caught Grace's wide eyes as conversation filled the air around them. She mouthed "Your Grace," her eyes searching his. His heart sank and his gut clenched. She'd learned the truth about his identity before he'd been able to explain it to her personally. He should have gone back out onto the terrace to have a private conversation with her. He tried to extricate himself from the neighbors and townspeople who surrounded him. He was stuck, with no ability to exit the crowd.

More people pressed around them, asking him one question after another. He did his best to smile while giving answers, though he wanted nothing more than to dismiss the entire room and go back to talking with Grace as he had only a few moments before.

CHAPTER EIGHTEEN

Grace was frozen to the floor as the word "grace" was used, not as her Christian name, but as Ollie's title. Grace tried to comprehend the situation, but shock filled her senses, muddling her brain. She had just danced with the duke. *The duke.* Ollie was the duke? Pain filled her as she felt the betrayal. He was supposed to be her friend—her confidant.

But all along he'd lied to her.

Heat drained from her head, a dizzy, nauseous feeling taking its place. She felt as though she might be sick.

Backing away from the group she maneuvered her way toward the door, away from Ollie—the duke.

She covered her head in her hands. She'd told him about her plans to make an advantageous match with the *duke.* *With him.* Had he been laughing at her this whole time?

"You've created quite the splash," Susan said, coming next to Grace, and looping an arm through hers. "You must tell me all about dancing with the duke."

Grace opened her mouth, then closed it again. How could she explain?

Susan raised an eyebrow. "Cousin? Are you unwell?"

Grace tried to draw in a deep breath, but the motion came in rapid shallow gasps instead. "I fear the ball is too stuffy for me," she said.

"Is it your ankle?" she asked in a concerned tone. "I was afraid you might dance to the point of fatigue."

Grace shook her head but could not muster up the energy to respond.

"Oh, you poor dear," Susan said, supporting Grace as they walked through the hallway toward the entrance. "We can go. There are plenty of carriages to take the other guests home. They will all be leaving at different times. We do not have to stay."

Grace smiled as best she could, forcing her cheek muscles to create a happy expression, instead of a scowl. She didn't want to take her cousin away from the ball because she was the hostess of the house party, but she couldn't stay at the ball any longer. Not with waves of humiliation crashing against her and threatening to drown her. She found her voice, and it sounded weary to her own ears. "That is kind of you, Susan. I should like to go home and retire for the evening. Please don't feel like you must accompany me back."

Susan asked for their wraps and ordered their carriage. "Do not be silly, Grace. I wouldn't leave you. I will order a tray to your room in the morning, and you may sleep as long as you choose so you can recover from the exercise."

Grace nodded. Susan only saw Grace's fatigue as a physical burden, but it was the rest of Grace that needed to recover. Grace kept her head in her hands on the drive home, her head spinning around Ollie. Susan didn't press her for details, only helped her up to her room when they arrived at home. She took the initiative in ordering the tray and pulling the bell pull to have Molly come and attend to Grace.

"Please send for me if you need anything," Susan said. "I'm sure a full night's rest will do wonders for you."

"Thank you, Susan, you are most attentive," Grace said.

Susan left the room, and Grace immediately put her hands over her face again. "Oh, what must he think of me?" she whispered to herself. Her cheeks heated as she remembered with very great details all the things she'd said to Ollie—to *the duke*—all when she had no idea who he really was. Mortification rose inside of her. A dread that left each of her nerves raw.

Earlier this evening she had contemplated what it would be like to pursue a relationship with Ollie, instead of the duke. But now, only one thing was certain in her mind—she now didn't have the option to pursue Ollie or the duke... they were the same person. She closed her eyes to the harsh reality of her predicament. She'd made an even bigger fool of herself in front of Ollie than simply riding out unattended in the forest. And because of that she'd ruined everything.

Ollie being the duke could have seemed like an answer to all her problems. Hadn't she wondered what life could be like with Ollie before she found out? Yes, but it didn't matter. She'd told Ollie as much on two separate occasions.

He'd been supportive of her pursuing the duke, but that was now a complete impossibility. The sooner she left this ball and this house party the better. It was humiliating to think of all that she had told Ollie about her plans.

She should vacate her cousin's house immediately, but there was still a full week left of the house party. She thought of all the other gentlemen in attendance. She'd been polite to each of them, but she hadn't really encouraged any of their attentions. Was there time to change that? Would a week be enough time to create a new impression?

Would her family find another match acceptable if it wasn't the duke?

She hoped so, because now she had no choice.

Hot, angry tears spilled onto her cheeks. He'd lied to her. She squeezed her eyes shut, willing the humiliation to disperse, but it continued to cling to her, like unrelenting tree branches in the woods.

She shook her head furiously. She needed a new course. She didn't need to fall in love with someone else at the house party. What a silly notion it was to let her heart get involved at all.

"I've forgotten my whole purpose," she said to the empty room. "I will do my duty and hope for the best." She needed to make a smart match, an advantageous match.

Just because she'd learned what it meant to love someone, didn't mean that she had to think on that while she married to help her family. Love meant embarrassment and mortification. Love meant she was vulnerable to her feelings of the heart, and none of those things would serve her. She knew she wouldn't be able to forget what love felt like, but it wouldn't be her focus. She couldn't risk it. She only needed to make an acceptable match, without any interference from her heart. Love was a terrible game, and one that she'd just lost at.

A KNOCK SOUNDED AT THE DOOR, AND SUSAN STEPPED inside before Grace said anything.

"Grace, are you still unwell?" Susan surveyed the untouched tray on the desk.

Grace forced a smile. "I am perfectly well," she said, doing her best to believe her own words. "I plan to join in the festivities this afternoon." She needed to start making an effort with other gentlemen in the party.

Susan's brow wrinkled with confusion. "I am glad to see that you are recovering, but why did you send the duke away this morning? He called on you very particularly."

Grace opened her mouth to speak but no words came out.

"What it is, Grace? Did you not enjoy dancing with him last night? The two of you looked very happy during your set."

"I did enjoy dancing with him," she said truthfully. "Though that was before I knew who he was."

"What do you mean?"

"I mean, I did not know that he was the duke when I began dancing with him."

Susan blanched. "Surely you were introduced before dancing."

Grace bit her lip, wondering how much she dare tell her cousin. She wanted to tell Susan about her time in the woods with Ollie—about everything that had happened between her and the duke. But she didn't know how to start. All her thoughts were too jumbled, too tangled to make sense.

"The duke has paid you a great compliment, first in his attentions toward you at the ball, and now to call on you. Do you not see the significance of that?"

Grace closed her eyes. Her cousin made valid points. "It is more complicated than it appears on the surface."

"I do not see how that is possible." Susan studied her for a moment, then handed Grace a small, white handkerchief. "This is for you."

Grace opened the handkerchief, her fingers trembling as

she pulled out her mother's silver comb. She blinked. "I thought I'd lost it. Where did you find it?" She had looked through her saddlebags several times but had been disappointed.

"The duke left it for you." Susan raised an eyebrow. "I do not remember it being in your hair yesterday."

Grace leaned against the frame of her bed and sighed. She wanted to tell her cousin all about the duke, and this was the opening she needed. "I have a story to tell you," she said. "It may take me a few tries to compose all of my ideas, but please let me finish before you say anything."

Susan nodded and sat on the bed next to Grace, looking expectantly.

Grace took a steadying breath and began. She told Susan everything, from the time she left the ill Mrs. Mead and her daughters to her accident in the woods, to her subsequent rescue by Ollie.

She could tell from Susan's expression that she wanted to say something, but Grace pushed on. She recounted the entirety of their time together in the woods, emphasizing the fact that neither of them had come away from the experience with a tarnished reputation. She told Susan about their conversations, and all that she had told Ollie about her family circumstances.

Then she told her cousin about their dance in the cottage, his tenderness toward her, and his help in making sure that she arrived safely at Susan's residence.

She finished her story with all the details of their time together, and when she was finished, she looked to her cousin. "That is why I left last night after the dance. I found out he was the duke when the group formed around us."

Susan blew out a breath. "That is a lot to take in. But surely, this is not a bad situation. After all, you came to this house party with the idea to make a match with the duke. And, as it turns out, you've done so, although in a most unconventional way."

A warning voice sounded in Grace's head. "If anyone were to find out about this, it would harm our reputations."

Susan waved her hand in the air dismissively. "Your secret is safe with me, Grace. Have no fear of that. I only meant that it seems that the duke returns your feelings."

Grace shook her head. "Do you not see how mortifying this is, Susan? I told him all my plans. I told him about my family situation. I had no intention of revealing that to anyone at the house party. I would have never told him if I'd known he was the duke." Heat flooded her cheeks, scorching her skin with the reminder that she'd been too outspoken with Ollie.

"It is not so hopeless. He did come calling on you."

"I do not want to see him again, Susan. The embarrassment alone is enough to cause me to faint."

Susan offered her a small smile. "It truly cannot be as bad as all that. It sounds like the two of you have a connection. And considering that he has been a widower for five years, and to my knowledge has never once called on a single female during that time—that is something."

It was something—but it was something that didn't matter—or shouldn't matter at least.

Oliver slapped his hand against his thigh as he walked away from Penrose Hall. It was the second day that he'd been refused when calling on Grace. Frustration poured through him as he trudged down the steps, waiting for his horse.

He swallowed. He'd brought this on himself. He hadn't lied to her directly, but he'd reserved some of the truth back. Judging by his dismissal two days in a row, it was clear that Grace did not want to see him. But he couldn't fix things between them, if he wasn't allowed the opportunity to at least speak to her.

He should have thought this through better. A groomsman led Poseidon toward him. Oliver patted Poseidon's neck. It was time for a long ride. He mounted his horse but kept Poseidon's pace sedate as he directed his horse on the long drive. Once he reached the fields, he would let him run to his heart's content. Hopefully it would do him some good too.

Behind him he heard a voice, calling him. His heart lurched. Had Grace changed her mind? But when he looked back, it was not Grace who was running down the steps, but her cousin.

"Your Grace," Lady Elliott said, through panting breaths. "I'm so glad I caught you."

Oliver stopped in front of her and dismounted, holding onto Poseidon's reins. He bowed. "Lady Elliott." He wasn't sure what else to say. After all, she was the one coming outside to talk with him. It was clear there was something on her mind. And he didn't wait long for an answer.

"I apologize that my cousin is not up for callers again today."

Oliver nodded. "You have nothing to apologize for."

"She really is a sweet girl, with a very kind temperament," Lady Elliott said, her face showing her distress.

Oliver smiled. He knew both of those things. He also knew that Grace had a fire within her. That zeal for life was something that had intrigued him from the very beginning. She was determined and selfless. But he couldn't tell Lady Elliott that he knew those traits and more about Grace. He settled on the response that he could give. "I believe it."

"We didn't know you had returned so soon from your travels. I had assumed you were still out of town."

Oliver could see the confusion in the woman's eyes. He

did his best to allay her feelings. "I apologize. I returned earlier than expected but felt it would be inconsiderate and presumptuous to assume that my spot was still available when I had already given my response previously. I hope you know that it had nothing to do with you or your house party. I am still ..."

"Grieving," she supplied the word.

He paused before responding. Previously, when he'd wanted to get out of engagements and social functions, it had been easy for him to rely on the crutch that he'd still needed time to grieve the unfortunate accident and death of his wife a few years before. But that wasn't the reason now. He could see that he'd carried around that sentiment for longer than he'd needed to. It was the easy excuse—the one that wasn't questioned. Perhaps it had been a long time since the excuse applied to him.

But meeting Grace—developing feelings for Grace—had proven to him that his heart wasn't the irreparable organ he'd thought it to be. He'd found laughter with Grace, hope with Grace, and not merely for show in social settings where it was expected that he would laugh and dance and entertain. No. With Grace it wasn't for anything like that.

"Lady Elliott, I believe that five years of being a widower has indeed been enough time in my grief. I believe I have come out of it."

Her eyebrows shot up. "Truly, Your Grace?"

He nodded. "I am only trying to figure out how to begin ... socializing ... again." He looked at the house, toward the door where he'd called twice and been rejected twice. "It appears that so far I do not know precisely how to go about it."

Lady Elliott gave him a sympathetic look. "My cousin is not usually one to turn away callers," she said, following his gaze. "I believe she must really not feel up to company. I do not think you should give up so easily."

It was clear Lady Elliott did not know the full story between him and Grace—or rather, between "Ollie" and Grace. "Do you have another suggestion aside from calling on her?" he asked, wondering if there was a different way to be in company with Grace. He already felt like an intruder trying to call on her in the middle of a house party. As he thought about it, it wasn't particularly polite. Perhaps what he needed was some patience. If he waited until after the house party ended, it might be easier to gain her attention.

"Why don't you come for dinner and join us for the rest of the house party?" Lady Elliott asked.

Oliver was not trying to beg an invitation, nor did he want to put Grace out if she truly did not wish to see him.

Sensing his hesitation, Lady Elliott spoke again. "Or perhaps that is too many social engagements to commit to. How about coming for one dinner and our musicale evening?"

"I should not wish to inconvenience you," he said. "Indeed, I do not want to complicate your plans."

"You would be most welcome, and it would be no trouble at all to have you attend for an evening. A musicale is not like an evening of cards or games where the numbers need to be even. And those evenings are still negotiable. Even when planning perfectly, not everyone engages in every activity I plan."

Oliver was still nervous about intruding, but after Lady Elliott expressed how much she would like to have him join in, he relented. After all, if things went awry, he could always excuse himself from the party early. And the party would be large enough that if Grace wanted to, she could spend the entire evening talking with others. "I believe that is the best course of action," he said with determination.

Lady Elliott clapped her hands together. "Splendid! I am so glad to hear it. Our musicale is scheduled for tomorrow evening. Dinner will be served at six."

Oliver nodded. "I shall be there. Thank you, Lady Elliott."

CHAPTER TWENTY

Grace spoke with Lord Stanton in the drawing room before dinner. She'd spent her free time over the last few days playing her piano piece for tonight's musicale, which was to begin directly after dinner. Lord Stanton spoke about his lands and his house. Again. Grace nodded, trying to ask thoughtful questions about the same topics, though she felt as though she ran out of questions about gardens and grounds two days previous.

A knock sounded at the drawing room door, and the butler pushed out his chest with pomp. "His Grace, the Duke of Norfolk."

Grace turned toward the door. She had to be dreaming. After two days of calling on her in a row, he'd not come again that morning. Not that it mattered as she had it in her to refuse the man a third time. But here he was entering the drawing room, dressed for dinner.

She briefly caught her cousin's eye. Susan smiled, but then turned her attention to the duke, as if she'd been expecting him.

Susan spoke to the whole room. "We are so pleased to have the Duke of Norfolk join us this evening. His Grace was originally out of town and unable to attend the whole of our house party, but as he was able to finish his urgent matters earlier than planned and attend our events tonight." Susan went on making the personal introductions.

Grace couldn't remove her eyes from the duke as he was introduced. He walked around the room, carrying himself with a presence that extended beyond his person. He was every bit the picture of strength and refinement. How had she ever thought he was simply a woodman in the forest, a man of no consequence?

They stopped in front of her and Lord Stanton. Susan introduced Lord Stanton to the duke first, and then turned to Grace.

"And though you have already met, allow me to formally introduce my cousin to you, Your Grace. This is Miss Campbell. Cousin, this is my neighbor, Oliver Hayward, Duke of Norfolk."

He bowed. His eyes never left hers.

Heat threatened to rush to her face and suddenly breathing felt difficult.

"It is a pleasure to see you again, Miss Campbell," he said, taking her hand in his and squeezing it gently. Then he brought her hand to his lips and kissed it gently.

The contact sent scorching heat up her arm. The touch nearly undid her. Grace had been so used to the way he said her Christian name, that the use of her surname sounded completely foreign to her. "Your Grace," she said, bobbing a small curtsy before her eyes found his again.

"May I say that the comb looks beautiful in your hair," he said.

Grace's hand immediately touched the jeweled ornament. "Thank you." She should thank him for returning it to her, but she didn't want to say it with so many listening ears around. "I thought I had lost it."

He lowered his voice, his words so quiet they only reached her ears. "It was not lost, only left on the small table by the mirror."

"It means a lot to me," she said, conflicting emotions inside her. "Thank you."

Before she had time to be too uncomfortable from the introduction—and their closeness—dinner was announced. Lord Stanton held out his arm to Grace, and she took it, all the while watching as her cousin, the hostess, went into dinner on the duke's arm.

Lady Elliott had made it a matter of priority not to stand on ceremony during the house party, so that each guest had the opportunity to sit next to new people at every meal. The system had been brilliant. Until now. Lord Stanton made it a point to sit close to the duke. In fact, he was only two seats away. And Grace was in the middle.

Grace caught her cousin's eye more than once, but

Susan only seemed to smile during dinner, and gave no indication that she understood just how uncomfortable Grace was.

"I am glad to see you are well," the duke said, sincerity filling each word.

Grace just about dropped her soup spoon. Talking about her injured ankle would be completely inappropriate at the table. She lowered her voice. "As you see, Your Grace. I told you as much when we were dancing that I am quite recovered."

He tilted his head to the side, amusement flickering in them. "I meant about the previous two mornings when you were not up for callers. I hope you are feeling better now."

Heat burned her cheeks, and she wanted to blame the soup for their sudden rise in temperature. "Quite, Your Grace. Is there something you particularly wanted to discuss with me?"

"As a matter of fact there is something quite delicate in nature that I wish to speak to you about." His eyes pleaded with her, begging her not to turn him down.

She could not have such a discussion at the table. It would be overheard. She lowered her voice. "Not here."

"Very well. When would be convenient for you?"

Grace widened her eyes. "I cannot think of a time that would be convenient at all, Your Grace."

"Please, Grace," he said, whispering her Christian name so softly, she almost missed it.

Grace gave one brief nod, unable to speak words through her emotions.

The dinner companion on the duke's other side captured the duke's attention, wanting opinions on the horses he was keeping, and Grace was left to think on what he could possibly wish to discuss with her.

Lord Stanton leaned over to Grace. "Are you distressed, Miss Campbell? You haven't touched the fish course."

Grace moved her fork around her plate, trying to make it look as if she'd made some sort of attempt to eat it, but at Lord Stanton's observation, she knew that she was doing a poor job, so she set down her fork and turned her entire attention over to Lord Stanton and his repetitive conversation for the remainder of the meal.

GRACE CAUGHT UP WITH SUSAN ON THE WAY INTO THE drawing room. Lowering her voice she said, "Cousin, you do not seem surprised that the Duke of Norfolk joined our party tonight."

Susan smiled at her. "Of course I'm not. I invited him. Did I not mention it? I extended the offer when he came calling yesterday."

Grace swallowed. "I was unaware that he would be here."

Susan gave her a knowing smile. "He will be staying for the musicale as well."

Grace drew in a sharp intake of breath. She gripped her cousin's arm harder at the news. "Please do not make me play first. I need time to compose myself."

Susan looked at her cousin in the eye, then gave a sharp nod. "Very well. I will move you in the programme. You may play fourth."

"Thank you," Grace said, barely managing to get the words out before Susan was off to the other side of the room, fussing about the pianoforte and sheets of music.

Lord Stanton found Grace and escorted her into the back row of chairs set for the musicale. "I look forward to hearing you play," he said, once he and Grace were settled into their chairs.

"I quite agree. I have it under very good authority that she sings like an angel when she plays the pianoforte," another voice said from the other side of Lord Stanton. It was none other than the duke.

Grace gulped, not knowing how she was going to calm her nerves. She was now more agitated, not less. Perhaps she should have just played first and gotten it over with, then begged to be excused. But it was too late now. The first woman sat on the bench in front of the ivory keys, looking toward the hostess for a cue of when to begin.

Susan was all smiles in front of the house party. She welcomed everyone with a gusto that didn't belie the fact that everyone in attendance had just eaten together. At the end of her prepared speech, she announced the order of the programme, and then said, "Lord Stanton, could we ask you if you would be so kind as to turn the pages for Miss Ramsey? It would be very much appreciated."

Miss Ramsey blushed, and Lord Stanton stood immediately and made his way to Miss Ramsey's side. As she began playing, Ollie—er, the duke—slid into Lord Stanton's vacant seat.

It took all of Grace's composure not to yelp aloud. "What are you doing?" she whispered.

Ollie smiled. "Enjoying the company of a beautiful woman next to me."

Grace stared forward, unwilling to respond. She tried to focus on the way Miss Ramsey played her scales throughout the piece.

"I have much to say to you, Grace."

She only shook her head.

"Please," he said, his voice a whisper.

Grace whispered through tight lips. "Everyone will hear our conversation."

Miss Ramsey finished her piece and the room filled with applause. Lord Stanton escorted Miss Ramsey to a chair, and Grace assumed that he would come back and rescue her from having to sit next to the duke for the duration of the programme. But Lord Stanton simply helped the next young woman to the pianoforte and turned pages for her as well. So, she would not find help from Lord Stanton until it was her turn to play.

At that the duke leaned closer as the second piece

started, his lips hovering just above her ear. He spoke softly. "Is this better?"

The air from his breath tickled her neck. It was definitely not better. She didn't respond, only kept her eyes trained toward the pianoforte. But it was impossible to pay attention to anything except Ollie next to her.

"Why did you not receive me when I called on you?"

Grace turned toward him. This was the question he'd wanted to know? She had spent the entire dinner hour fretting about what he was going to say, and this was how he started out? A wave of embarrassment filled her, unwilling to let her go. "Why didn't you tell me who you really are?" It could have saved her feeling humiliated. Embarrassment still burned in her.

"I did try to, but there was never a good time," he said, looking a little uncomfortable.

"You had the chance to tell me on the terrace, or on the dance floor, and you didn't." Not to mention they'd had days of talking at the hunting lodge with no one else to interrupt their conversation.

"How could I show up as the duke when you invited Ollie?" he whispered back.

"It would have taken less than ten words to explain. You had ample opportunities."

"I apologize. I didn't want to let the moment go."

"What is that supposed to mean?"

"It means I really liked being just Ollie around you, not the duke."

"That's ridiculous. You *are* the duke. You were the duke the whole time."

"Yes, but you didn't know that. And it was refreshing to be seen in a true light."

Swirls of emotion spun around her like snow falling in a storm. She was disoriented. She'd spend almost the whole of the time in the cabin vocally processing her plan to impress the duke. She wanted to run away from this moment, to find somewhere to hide. "Were you laughing at me the whole time? For all the women that throw themselves at you?"

The duke did not answer right away. And Grace knew she already knew the answer.

Before he responded, the piece ended, and Lord Stanton made his way over to her row, waiting for her to come to the aisle, and then he escorted her to the bench.

Grace was grateful for the muscle memory that took over as her fingers touched the keys. She didn't sing. She couldn't trust her own voice.

Lord Stanton turned the pages too early, but it didn't matter. She'd committed this piece to memory already. She stumbled over her notes only when she looked up to see the duke's eyes watching her intently.

After that she focused on the notes on the sheets in front of her. They swam around on the page as she concentrated on not lifting her eyes from them.

When she finished the piece, she curtsied, and then Lord Stanton escorted her back to the row she'd been on, and left her to help the next young woman.

Instead of sitting down, she went to where Susan sat and let her know that she needed some fresh air for a moment but would return shortly. Her cousin nodded, and Grace took the liberty of letting herself onto the balcony from the back of room.

The air was frigid, pouring a cool calm into her. The drawing room had been far too stuffy. Far too many emotions ...

The door clicked behind her, but she kept her back to the door.

"You'll catch a cold out here in this kind of weather," the duke's voice said quietly behind her.

She didn't turn around, just gripped the edge of the balcony for strength. "I've survived worse."

A low chuckle sounded. "Touché, Grace."

A warm, tingling filled her as he used her Christian name once again. But hurt crept through. "You lied to me."

"Only indirectly."

She let out a mirthless laugh. "Should that make me feel better?"

"No. But I never said I wasn't the duke. I never tried to purposefully deceive you."

"The way you talked about the duke ..."

"It was unfair and deceptive. And there is no excuse for it, except to say that I had to keep my guard up at that point."

"Your guard up, against a woman?"

He came closer. "Yes. After all you were open with your plans."

She covered her face with her hands. "You were laughing at me. You still are."

"Grace, please look at me. I deeply and sincerely apologize for my behavior and for leading you on and not revealing my true identity sooner. But I wasn't laughing at you that day in the woods, or any of the other days since."

"I find that hard to believe, Your Grace." She knew things between them could never work. He'd been privy to her scheming plans and the fact still mortified her.

"I wasn't laughing at you, Grace," he said again, firmly. He put a hand on top of hers as it rested on the balcony. "I didn't come to call on you to laugh at you either. I came because I wanted to see you again. I wanted to explain in person."

Heat raced from where his hand covered hers, filling her with a familiar warmth in the cool evening air. "What did you want to explain?"

"I wanted to explain that I was trying to tell you who I was while we were dancing. That was what I wanted to talk to you about before we started dancing. I'm sorry, Grace."

"I accept your apology, but where does that leave us? You know all of my secrets. My intents."

"And I saw you conflicted about those intents. You cared for me—for Ollie—even when you made presumptions about my circumstance."

"I didn't mean to," she said. "I wasn't trying to form a connection with anyone before I met *the duke*."

One corner of his lips quirked upwards. "And that is why I think we are right for each other—why I came calling on you after the ball. Fate brought me to you that day in the woods. I found you, Grace, and in turn I found grace in my life."

She swallowed. "I do not understand."

"I was mourning and grieving over a life that wasn't mine anymore. And then I found you. And you changed me. In such a short time. You helped me see that there was more to life ... more that I didn't want to miss out on again."

"Why would you want me, when you could have your pick of anyone?"

"Because you came into my life for a reason. You brought a hope into my life that wasn't there before. You once said that if you had the ability to choose, you would want nothing more than to consider me a suitor. Did you mean that? Or were you simply saying the things a poor man in the woods would want to hear from a beautiful woman?"

A small smile formed on her lips, melting away the earlier anxieties she'd held onto. Ollie was using her own words to make his case. He was asking in earnestness. And she had this moment to choose exactly what she wanted for her life. Confusion and embarrassment whipped away from her in the wind, and she was left with clarity. "I think you know me well enough to believe that I have always spoken the truth with you. I have always been open with you, even about my mislaid plans. I meant it then, and I still mean it now."

He squeezed her hand, lifting it up and holding it in both of his. "Then trust that I also mean what I say, when I tell you that your openness is one of the things I admire about you."

"I developed feelings for you when I didn't know you were a duke, but I told you all about how I was planning to win over the duke. Do you not find that strange and slightly off-putting?" she asked, wanting to hear his reassuring words.

"Off-putting? You? I would never think such a thing. Quite the contrary, I believe you falling for me when you knew me simply as Ollie is a much greater compliment than you trying to win me over as a duke. I fell for the woman who saw me for who I really am." He wrapped his arms around her, pulling her closer.

She stayed in his arms, feeling his warmth and strength. "You did save my life, perhaps that is the reason I first fell in love with Ollie," she whispered.

An understanding passed between them. Ollie's blue eyes darkened with determination as he glanced at her lips. He searched her eyes for acceptance, and perhaps permission. Grace smiled and leaned the slightest amount closer to him.

He kissed her gently, his lips exploring hers. Warmth and heat spread through her, banishing the chilly evening.

When they broke the kiss, he said, "I did save your life, but in the process, you've saved mine as well."

Love and excitement for their future encompassed Grace as she embraced the man in front of her. With her arms around his neck, she pulled him closer, drinking in more of his kisses.

"You know, if we get caught out here, you would be forced to marry me to save my reputation," she said softly, laughing at the thought.

"What was it you said? It wouldn't be the worst thing." He smiled at her. "But I do prefer to court you properly and prove to you that I can be the man in your life that will make you happy."

"I already know that about you. I knew it from the first day at your cottage."

"It's actually a hunting lodge," he said, smiling.

"Very well, I suppose that does make much more sense now."

"I love you," he said. "And I'm going to spend the rest of my days making sure you know how much it means to have you in my life, Grace."

"I love you, Ollie," she said, whispering the words against his lips and kissing him again.

EPILOGUE

PENROSE HALL - ONE MONTH LATER

Conversation surrounded Grace as her maid attended to her hair. Susan's largest guest room was barely large enough to hold everyone, but Grace wouldn't have it any other way. Her sisters helped one another with their hairstyles, reminding Grace of times back in her childhood home, Cherrywood Manor. Her mother oversaw the progress, and Grace observed everything from where she sat in front of the glass.

The past month had been a whirlwind of wedding preparations and ordering new gowns for the upcoming London Season. Grace and Oliver had written to her parents, and they'd come to Penrose Hall immediately with all of Grace's younger sisters. Her father gave his consent to the union immediately upon arrival after meeting with the Duke of Norfolk.

Susan had graciously agreed to host her relations while

the banns were read for three weeks. The time had flown, with each day requiring new decisions to be made. And each day Oliver spent time with Grace and her family. He'd written to his mother and sisters, but with them overseas they wouldn't receive the message until after the wedding.

"A winter wedding. It's like something out of a fairytale." Harmony clasped her hands to her chest and sighed.

"It is a beautiful time of year," Patience agreed. "But it makes for cold traveling for your wedding trip."

"She won't be cold. Did you not see how many capes and cloaks she has, Patience?" Charity asked. "She will be perfectly comfortable and fashionable on her wedding trip."

Grace laughed. Charity often thought of fashion. "We shall go on a short wedding trip now, and then we will plan something grander after the London Season is complete. The duke is required to attend Parliament, so we do not have much time for travel, even if the roads and weather were nicer."

"I suppose that makes sense," Hope chimed in. "A shorter wedding trip now is much more desirable than waiting until after the London Season to wed."

"Indeed. And London will also be a great adventure."

"I'm glad you will be coming to London," Felicity said. "I was so hoping we would see more family there."

"The fortunate thing about being a twin is that you are always with a sister," Grace reminded her.

Faith nodded. "It is true, but I agree with Felicity. It will be more enjoyable to have you along with us."

Grace's maid finished arranging the last of her curls on top of her head. The silver and gold circlet woven in her hair sparkled when it caught the light.

Her mother smiled at her. "I see you've decided to wear the comb in your hair too."

Grace touched the back of her head, where the comb was intertwined with the curls. "It brought me luck. I can't imagine wearing anything else."

"It suits you. You look beautiful," her mother said, resting her hands upon Grace's shoulders. "I'm so proud of you and the woman you've become."

"Thank you, Mama," Grace said.

"You look exactly like an angel," Harmony said.

Each sister embraced Grace in turn before filing out the bedroom door to depart for the parish.

Harmony fell into step with Grace as they descended the stairs. "Being a duchess sounds very romantic."

Grace put an arm around her youngest sister, briefly squeezing the girl to her side. "It does sound romantic, but more than anything it's romantic to marry someone you love."

"Do you love the Duke?" Harmony asked.

Grace smiled at her sister. Warmth filled her at the mention of love. "Very much. And falling in love with him had nothing to do with his wealth or his status."

Charity, who was ahead of Grace and Harmony on the

stairs, turned back. "That is quite remarkable, but I suppose it is hard to know if those things have no bearing on one's decision to marry."

Grace smiled. "In this case, I know with complete certainty that material comforts didn't influence my love for him."

"You will be very happy then, no matter what comes into your life," Faith said, joining in the conversation.

"I believe I will," Grace said.

***

The ceremony was brief, the vows beautiful. Grace looked at the man next to her and was filled with love and hope for the future. Standing next to her, Oliver was more than she could have imagined for herself, and everything that she desired. He was thoughtful, kind, and she wanted to spend every day for the rest of her life with this remarkable man.

The world faded around them as she focused on the love of her life, and the journey that brought them to this moment.

As the vicar pronounced their marriage, Oliver took her in his arms and kissed her. Heat flooded her center at his touch. The look in his eyes when they parted left her feeling loved and cherished in a way she'd never experienced before.

***

After the wedding, the family made their way back to Cliffton Manor where a large wedding breakfast was provided.

Though Grace sat next to her husband, they were pulled into conversations with other family members. She rested her hand in his beneath the table. The way Oliver conversed so easily with her family made it feel as if he'd always known each of them personally. The idea warmed Grace's heart.

Oliver turned to Faith. "Are you looking forward to the London Season?"

Faith gave him a small smile. "I think so."

Grace could sense some apprehension from her sister, but that was not like her at all.

Harmony spoke from across the table. "Will you come see the cherry blossoms this year?"

Before Grace could answer, Oliver spoke up. "Yes, Harmony, we plan to come to Cherrywood Manor after our wedding trip, right before we go to London for the Season."

Grace turned to her husband. "Are you sure we have time for a visit?"

Oliver squeezed her hand. "Of course, my love."

Grace turned back to Harmony. "We wouldn't miss it."

Harmony smiled, but her attention was focused on the duke. "I can't wait to show you my favorite spots."

Oliver chuckled. "I should love a tour."

Harmony beamed. "I can show you everything."

After the meal, Grace caught up with Faith and pulled out the comb from her hair.

"What are you doing? You'll ruin your hair."

Grace smiled. "The hairstyle is still holding," she said. Besides it had been through much worse, and Oliver had seen that already. She put the comb into her sister's hand.

Faith blinked. "What is this for? Mama gave it to you."

"It has served its purpose and provided me luck. Now it's your turn. Take it with you to London. And don't fret. You are going to have an enjoyable time during the Season."

Faith nodded, her eyes becoming moist at the corners. "Thank you, Grace," she whispered. She opened her hand and studied the beautiful comb. "I shall treasure it and wear it often."

"I would suggest you do. You never know, you might be wearing it when you meet your future husband."

Faith smiled but the gesture looked forced. Finally, she said, "I shall do my best not to disappoint the family."

Grace put her arms around her sister. "You are not a disappointment. And nothing you do or fail to do will change that."

"Thank you, Grace."

***

Three days later, the Duke and Duchess of Norfolk started on their wedding trip. In the winter their traveling was limited, but Oliver wanted to take a trip before they spent the Season in London.

As the ducal carriage stopped, Grace asked, "Are we at

the inn already? That was a much faster trip than I expected."

"We have a detour."

"A detour? Are we lost?"

"Quite the contrary, we are exactly where we should be." He opened the door of the carriage and helped her down.

"The cottage?" She looked out in wonder.

"Its proper name is the Norfolk Hunting Lodge."

She smiled. "I think I shall always think of it as Ollie's Cottage."

"You'll have to think of it a little differently."

"Why is that? I like the name cottage."

"It is no longer just *my* cottage, my love. It is *our* cottage. I thought we might want to stay a few nights. If nothing else we can grab the book of sonnets to bring with us."

Grace laughed. "I wonder that you didn't suggest the book on botany. After all, you have most of the sonnets committed to memory. I watched you recite them by heart."

He picked her up and carried her toward the front door.

She squealed in surprise. "I do not need to be carried anymore. I am not a wilting daisy. My ankles have been working properly."

He held her close to him, loving the way she fit into his arms, and into his life. "But what if I want to carry you?"

She held his neck tightly. "I suppose it is not improper for a husband to carry his wife."

"Indeed it is not."

"Very well, I will allow it."

He held her close, then kissed her before carrying her inside. He put her on the settee and began building a fire. "This feels very familiar," he said.

"Yes it does, but this time there is something different."

"Besides being my wife, you mean?"

She smiled. "Yes. This time you shall not beat me at checkers. I am determined to win at least one game."

Did you enjoy Finding Grace?

Please leave a review for Finding Grace on Amazon.
(*Other platforms also appreciated*).

It is one of the best ways to say thank you to an author!

Cheers!

Did you read James and Emma's story?

A woman determined to hide, a duke determined to fulfill his duty, and a London Season where neither expects to fall in love.

Start Reading The Duke's Secret now!

Cassandra's Story is next!
Order Unmasking the Marquess now!

A stolen kiss, a secret identity, and a thief that keeps the ton on its dance toes.

ENJOY A FREE EBOOK!

This Marriage of Convenience is anything but convenient.

Join Allie's Regency Reader's Club at

https://smarturl.it/alliefreebook

Join Allie's Regency Reader's Club for a free book, behind-the-scenes information, and exclusive bonus content!

See all of Allie's Books

ACKNOWLEDGMENTS

Finding Grace came together in a most serendipitous way. I'm so grateful to several people who helped this book come together so quickly!

First and foremost, I am grateful to my husband. He is my very own Mr. Darcy. He listened to me ramble on the way to a date night, talking about my brand new idea for a story. He brilliantly poked holes in my ideas, helping me to start with a strong outline, and has given me needed feedback and encouragement ever since. He's my favorite.

I received great feedback from the following beta readers: Donna C., Jennifer E., Susan G. Thank you to each of you for thoughtful feedback and quick turnaround time. I appreciate each one of you for helping to make this book better.

Though the story ideas are products of my imagination, my ideas and my stories are greatly enhanced by the friends who care deeply about my characters and give feedback that shapes my stories to be better than they would otherwise be. Specifically on this book the following helped and supported me in significant ways: Shawna, Tracy, Shelly, Ami, Stephanie, Kami, Danielle, and Kayla.

Special thanks to my mum. She's one of a kind, and life always looks brighter around her.

Special thanks to Monica H. and Mary E. who each named an estate in this book! You're both wonderful. Thank you!

Thank you to my readers and my reviewers. Your feedback and encouragement means the world to me. Thank you!

Finally, I'm grateful to my Heavenly Father, for the stories in my head and for the ability to put them down on paper and share them with others. I feel blessed to do this.

Cheers!

ABOUT ALLIE KENSINGTON

Once upon a time Allie fell in love, quite by accident. She was blinded by a deep friendship, which happened to be the perfect recipe for a love match to grow right under her nose, without her noticing.

The Regency era speaks to her with its rules, etiquette, and charm. Of course, the top hats and cravats are sure winners. She can quote the BBC version of Pride and Prejudice with 98% accuracy, plays the pianoforte with moderate proficiency, and has an affinity for the beneficial exercise of walking.

Allie is a famous author—*at least in her own home*—where her very own Mr. Darcy dotes on her and where their children play without the supervision of a governess.

Allie loves to connect with her readers! (It makes the long hours of typing in isolation worth it!).

Did you enjoy this Book?

Please leave a review for

Find Grace

on Amazon.

It will make my day!

It's the best way you can say thank you to an author!

Cheers!

Made in the USA
Middletown, DE
22 April 2023